THE
STONE
VEIL

THE STONE VEIL

Ronald Tierney

St. Martin's Press / New York

Library of Congress Cataloging-in-Publication Data

Tierney, Ronald.
    The stone veil.
      p.   cm.
    "A Thomas Dunne book."
    ISBN 0-312-03940-9
    I. Title.
PS3570.I3325S7   1990   813'.54—dc20   89-48532

First Edition

10 9 8 7 6 5 4 3 2 1

*Thanks to a supportive family
and to Douglas Varchol
and T. Thompson-Moore*

THE
STONE
VEIL

1

He thought about throwing her out. He wasn't listening anymore, anyway. There was some red-headed Irishman on the tube in oversized boxing shorts, slugging the hell out of some black guy. It was a bad fight. A street-level brawl pretending to be a boxing match.

"Would you please turn that off? I am doing my level best to hire you. Can't you even pretend to be interested?" demanded the woman, who dressed like she didn't belong anywhere in this neighborhood.

"How'd you get my name?" Shanahan asked, watching the black guy lose his mouthpiece. Lucky it wasn't his teeth. The black boxer's eyes widened. The red-headed guy moved in on him like a dumb, determined machine.

The woman fidgeted with the straps of her purse. "That's my business."

"No, that's my business. That's why I asked."

"You want a job or not?" she said, looking around the makeshift office that obviously doubled as his living room. She moved her foot to nudge away Shanahan's overattentive cat.

"I really don't give a shit." Finally the black guy began to box. A left, right, left uppercut, then a right, down across the Irishman's temple, all of it choreographed real quick and real smooth. Shanahan liked the black guy. When the guy got mad, he got smart.

"The Yellow Pages," the woman said.

Shanahan had almost forgotten she was there.

"I'm not in the Yellow Pages. I don't advertise. I don't have to. I'm independently poor. Look, it's time for me to feed the dog."

"The Ouija board."

"The what?"

"Your name came to me through the Ouija board."

All the white guy knew how to do was charge and throw punches. The jackhammer approach. But the black guy was bobbing, weaving, going in with combinations and backing away, bouncing high on his feet. By rights, Shanahan ought to have been for the Irishman. After all, Shanahan was Irish. Half Irish, anyway. And half German. Shanahan always professed to have inherited the German intelligence and the Irish inability to deal with it. Both birthrights exhibited a certain stubbornness, to the point of self-destruction if need be—and so did he. Even so, Shanahan hoped the white guy would bite the canvas. Knowing how to box was a gift, an art. Having a rock jaw and a mean streak didn't cut it.

"Say again," Shanahan said to the lady.

"The Ouija board. You do know what that is?"

"Yeah." Shanahan turned, walked to the screen door that led out to the backyard and his garden. She followed halfway. Her snippy bravado shrank.

"I needed help," she said. "I didn't know what kind of help. A doctor, a psychiatrist maybe. A lawyer. I did something that I know you'll think is crazy. I asked the Ouija board. And it wasn't crazy. It spelled out *S-H-A-N-A-H-A-N*. I went to the telephone book. The white pages. But there were a number of Shanahans. So I went back to the board and asked for a first name. It spelled out *Deets*."

Shanahan winced. That was his nickname.

"The only thing near that," she continued, her eyes closed, "was Dietrich Shanahan. When I called, you answered, 'Shanahan Private Investigation.' It all seemed to make sense." Her eyes opened and she lowered herself into the overstuffed chair facing the television. "But it doesn't look too promising, does it?"

It didn't. Shanahan didn't care much for mysticism, and he cared even less for her. However, Shanahan was also bored silly. And he could have used the money. He was making it on his Army retirement check and the incredibly modest sum he received from Social Security. The house was paid for. The heating bills, on the other hand, would kill him. It was early May and he was still paying for the previous January. His car needed work. So did the roof. He wanted some things for his garden, particularly some Japanese irises. They were about five dollars each and he wanted fifty of them. Maybe some Siberians, too, for the foliage.

———

Shanahan looked out the door. Casey, sixty pounds of mongrel driven by a nose that could track a flea through the Sahara, planted his rear end where Shanahan wanted to plant a healthy clump of *Iris kaempheri*. Shanahan would change his tack.

"Why doesn't it look promising?"

She gathered her purse and started toward the door. "This just isn't what I expected." Would she cry? Shanahan hoped she wouldn't.

"You want a cigar?" Shanahan asked, thinking the non sequitur would either send her scurrying or stop her in her tracks.

She stopped, stunned. "What on earth are you talking about?"

"Just what *did* you expect?"

"Never mind." Her hand was on the doorknob. He was about to lose his flowers.

"Someone younger?"

"Frankly, Mr. Shanahan, yes, and someone a little more sympathetic. Someone at least moderately interested in doing the work he says he does. Maybe," she said, a cruel, brittle smile forming, "someone a little less retired."

The black guy on TV came down hard with a shot at the Irishman's ear and the dumb boxer just got dumber. He buckled, then crumbled onto the mat.

"Well, Mrs. . . . uh . . . I'm sorry." Shanahan almost meant it.

"See, you don't even remember my name, so how could you possibly . . ." She sputtered, finally getting out, "You're a very crude and insensitive man." She left.

Shanahan, who had her name on the strange little calling card she presented, would've made a pact with the devil for those irises, but he wasn't quite sure he could endure what's-her-name. The Irishman was down for the count.

"You deserve it," he said to the boxer struggling to get off the floor. The dog scratched at the screen door, then barked twice. Casey wanted in and he wanted to eat. Now.

"All right, Case. I screwed up. It's not that I don't like women. I just don't like women who don't like cats and purse their lips when they hear the word *shit*. Besides, her husband isn't missing. He's gone. Got smart." Shanahan followed Casey into the kitchen. "Went for a walk one day, thought about his life for the first time in twenty years, and decided not to come back."

———

Shanahan met Harry Stobart at the bar at 8:00 p.m., the usual time. Harry had been there a couple of hours already. He was lit.

"I hadda get a head start," Harry said. "I gotta leave by nine. The Cubs play L.A. and they are on a tear."

"Fish sandwich," Shanahan told the bartender, "if it's fresh."

"Caught it myself," said Delaney, the bartender, not bothering to look, just heading toward the kitchen.

"Swimming at the bottom of the freezer," Shanahan said.

"Onion?" Delaney called from the kitchen.

"Yeah," Shanahan said, shaking his head, thinking about the heartburn that would follow.

"Now that they got Dawson," Harry said, "could be the pennant. Maddux is gonna pitch tomorrow night. Don't wanna miss that one."

"Afraid I'll have to." Shanahan remembered his VCR, the one he got from the Hoffman case because Vince Hoffman didn't have the money to pay him. Shanahan had never bothered to hook it up. He had plenty of time to watch anything he wanted.

"What the hell you doin' more important than the Cubbies?" Harry asked.

"Something."

" 'Something,' the guy says. He's talkin' to Harry. Me. I tell this guy my deepest, innermost secrets and the guy answers 'something.' Christ be Jesus, Deets. This ain't the time to be keepin' secrets."

"Guy's got to have a few to keep him interesting," Shanahan said. "Besides, what deep dark secrets have you ever told me?"

"A man's got to be in the mood to tell them, Deets. You don't just tell 'em like that." Harry snapped his fingers.

"I'm not in the mood, Harry."

"You doin' a job?"

"No, something else." Then to change the subject, Shanahan told him about the lady and the Ouija board. "A Northside prissy thing. Gucci bag, Italian shoes. Wanted me to find her husband."

"Well?"

"I did the charitable thing. Looking at her, I figured the husband doesn't want to be found. Besides I'm getting too old for this shit." Harry stayed quiet. "The truth of the matter is I blew it. I didn't give a shit and it was pretty obvious."

The bartender put the plate in front of Shanahan, then a fork. A brown fish square on a plain bun, fries and a side dish of slaw.

"Christ, Delaney, that's quick," Shanahan said. "Dammit, you got a microwave."

"Times are changing, Deets. You change or you die."

"You die, no matter what," Harry said.

"I shouldn't have bought the damned thing," the bartender said.

"You damn right," Harry said. "Some things aren't supposed to change. Look at England. They've had the same damned queen for how many years?"

The bartender smiled nervously. He was a big man, about fifty, balding, with long strands of hair from the side pulled across the top of his forehead. Harry said that Delaney had a nose he couldn't have been born with. It took years to get it that pickled.

"What I mean to say, guys, is that I've sold the place." Delaney waited for a reaction. The reaction was a long, cold stare. "I figure one day, you know, a guy's gonna walk outta here and run over somebody, and somebody else is going to sue the hell out of me and there goes my retirement." More silence. "Look, I can't even afford the insurance rates. Even if I charged you guys two bucks a beer, I'm sinking. A guy made an offer, a good one. The neighborhood's changing, you know. And I hate to say this, but my clientele is either dying off or going to the home. You know?"

There were little knots of dough in the bun, grainy spots. Shanahan nibbled on some fries and drank his Miller out of the tall clear bottle.

———

"Change or die," that's what Delaney said. But Harry was right. Delaney was bowing out. What was the bartender going to do now? Find a little place in Florida and play bingo the rest of his life? But then, what was Shanahan doing? Sitting in a neighborhood bar every evening, listening to Harry's stories.

Shanahan drove his familiar route home. Habit. His life, through default, inertia, or lack of imagination had slipped into predictable patterns.

Was that so bad? Sitting around with Harry and a few cronies? Harry was entertaining. He was a good storyteller. It took Harry a long time to get started, but Harry built a story like you used to build a house. You dig for the basement, then the foundation, solid stuff. Houses with real wood and real stone. That's the way Harry told his stories, brick by brick, and then you were so caught up and laughing so hard you'd endure a bursting bladder just to hear the end. Yeah, there you were—two old men in a bar—killing time until it killed you.

"Change or die," the guy said. There was Maureen. She was something novel and unpredictable in Shanahan's life, wasn't she? Maybe he should have his head examined, but Maureen was what Shanahan was doing Tuesday night. It was none of Harry's business. But today was Monday. He'd watch the game, down a couple of J. W. Dant bourbons and mow the lawn in the morning.

———

Shanahan fell asleep halfway through the game. They were making a lot of errors, changing pitchers. The game seemed to go on forever. Stretched out on the sofa, he gave in early to leaden eyelids.

He usually slept well, if not long, and under just about any circumstances. He learned that in the trenches during World War II. Drafted at twenty-five. That made him senior among the eighteen-year-olds. They called him Dad, with some affection attached to the moniker.

After the war, he married, reenlisted, got Elaine pregnant, earned a few stripes, splitting his time between the Infantry and Intelligence. When Elaine gave birth, she named the kid Ty after Tyrone Power. Elaine had a crush on the actor. Starry-eyed, she used to say she fell for Shanahan because he looked as much like Tyrone Power as Tyrone Power did. Elaine stayed in Indianapolis, where her parents lived, and settled in this two-bedroom bungalow. Shanahan came home on leave periodically.

His son unfortunately came to view his father as an interloper. When Ty reached his teens he became unruly. So, while Shanahan worked out the last few years of his twenty-five-year Army hitch at Fort Leonard Wood, Missouri, preparing recruits for Vietnam, Elaine remained in Indianapolis. When Ty hit sixteen, he took off for San Francisco, probably tuning out or in or whatever they did on the corner of Haight and Ashbury.

Shanahan got out of the Army, finally moving into his own home. He did what many of the "non-coms" did with an intelligence background faced with the civilian job situation. He got his P.I. license. However, things started falling apart at home. Elaine had grown accustomed to Shanahan at a distance. She wasn't ready to have him around full time. Then, when a few hairs started showing on her upper lip, she panicked, fell in with her hair-burner and went off to tan her hide in the dry Phoenix sun.

Now he was dreaming of her. A bright sun, blue sky. Elaine stood out on the sidewalk, in front of the house. She was young, the age she was when they were married. She was smiling and waving. The phone was ringing inside. He tried to ignore it, but it wouldn't go away. Suddenly, he realized she was waving good-bye. He yelled, "Elaine, wait!" The dream went to black. Shanahan opened his eyes. He slowly became aware that the ringing came from the phone beside the couch.

"Yeah," he said groggily, his eyes catching the jagged black-and-white dots on the television screen.

"Mr. Shanahan?"

"Yeah."

"This is Mrs. Stone."

Silence.

"From this afternoon or, rather, yesterday afternoon, I guess it was."

Silence.

"Are you there?"

"No, I'm out playing tennis."

"I know I've awakened you. I am very sorry, but I couldn't sleep."

"I see, you thought I might want to share the experience."

"Please listen." She sounded frantic. "There's no one else I can turn to. I won't be able to sleep—or do anything else for that matter—unless you agree to help me."

"I never agree to anything when I'm drunk, sexually excited, or between the hours of midnight and dawn."

"May I stop by in the morning? Please, Mr. Shanahan."

"At your own risk," Shanahan replied. At the moment, he'd forfeit the flowers. The lady was a puddle. A genuine Northside neurotic.

"I'll take my chances," she said and hung up.

Some spunk after all. A spunky wacko, he thought, hanging up the phone. Somehow, he picked back up on the dream. It was the same lawn, the same sidewalk, the same sunny day. Only Elaine was gone. A clump of Japanese irises bloomed in the front yard. The phone was still ringing. His eyes opened in the darkness. It was the phone again. The real one.

"You're pressing your luck," he said.

"Dad?"

At first, Shanahan thought it was the wrong number, but then it was all clear to him. It was Ty calling him. Shanahan knew what the dream meant.

"Dad, this is Ty." The voice was embarrassed, tentative as if he was ready to hang up at any time. "I've booked a flight from Phoenix. I'll be in at four in the afternoon. Can I talk to you?"

"You don't have to come all this way to tell me. I know."

"You know? But it just happened."

"Elaine's dead, isn't she?"

"Yes, but how . . ."

Shanahan wanted to tell his son about the dream, but it all seemed too hard.

"Are you okay?" Shanahan asked. He couldn't help it; his voice was brittle, cold. He tried to soften it, but he knew he still sounded angry. "I mean about your mother." The words were okay. It was the tone that screwed things up. It was still the Army sergeant talking.

"I'm okay, Dad. We knew that it was . . . well, you know. How about . . ."

"I'm fine. These things happen. What is there to say?" Shanahan didn't know what to say. Ty had to be in his forties and a stranger. Shanahan cursed himself for sounding so damned distant, so removed. He was blowing it and there wasn't a fucking thing he could do.

"Yeah," his son said, coldly. "Yeah, no point. Well, I thought you ought to know. You had a right to know. I guess I could have dropped you a card."

The phone clicked suddenly.

"Dammit," Shanahan said, suddenly wide awake with much of the night still ahead of him.

2

At eight-thirty, Shanahan called Mrs. Stone. Whoever answered wasn't the lady of the house.

"I'm afraid Mrs. Stone isn't available at the moment," said the feminine voice.

"Please wake her up. Tell her it's Shanahan."

"She had a very long and upsetting night."

"So did I."

"May I take your number and have Mrs. Stone return the call when she awakes?"

"No."

"Then you'll call her—"

"No. You will go to where Mrs. Stone is dreaming about Ralph Lauren and gently tell her that Shanahan would like to have a word with her."

"Mr. Shanahan, I'm only the housekeeper and unless it is urgent, I have no intention of waking her up."

"Then I'm sure you'll find a way to explain that she has forfeited her right to the Publisher's Clearing House ten million dollar giveaway."

He heard her put the phone down. He waited.

Mrs. Stone's voice was weak. She coughed. "Yes."

"This is Shanahan."

"I was asleep."

"Well, that's the first good news I've had in twenty-four hours. I want to come over."

"We were to meet at your place, at eleven, I thought."

"I'll be there in half an hour. Does the housekeeper know about all of this?"

"Not all of it," Mrs. Stone said nervously.

"Then give her the day off. I don't want her around."

"Mr. Shanahan, why do you need to come here?"

"I'll be there the whole day. Going through every-thing. Everything, Mrs. Stone. Are you up to it?"

"Well, I suppose, if there's no other way."

"There's no other way," Shanahan said, looking down at the polite little business card she had handed him when they first met: MRS. WILLIAM B. STONE, VICE PRESIDENT OF THE INDIANAPOLIS JUNIOR LEAGUE, 14392 WINDING BEND ROAD. "How the hell do I find Winding Bend Road?"

"Do you know the Geist area?" she asked, apparently used to giving the directions.

———

Shanahan knew the Geist area or, rather, used to. The water company made a fortune off the huge city reservoir, selling small plots of land where the wealthy built expensive homes overlooking a mammoth man-made lake. He remembered when he and Elaine used to go there to get away from it all. Now when you go there you're in the thick of the burbs.

He had figured a half an hour, but he got lost in the maze of new homes and condos. Developers didn't make streets to get you from one place to another. They made streets so you could squeeze as many houses on them as possible. Amazing, people moved way out of the city only to be ten feet from their neighbors, all living on cul-de-sacs, as if privacy was important. It was more like forty-five minutes before his tan '76 Malibu pulled into the drive on Winding Bend.

His dog had made most of the trip with his head out of the window, ears swept back. Now, he was panting at the door, eager to get out.

"Be nice, Case. A lot of expensive furniture in there."

He and Casey knew each other pretty well. They'd been together for about three years. The dog liked to travel and just liked being with Shanahan. In fact, the dog picked Shanahan. One day Shanahan left his house to pick up his laundry, some liquor, and some cat litter and found the dog on his front lawn like he owned the place. Shanahan paid little attention. When he returned two hours later, the dog was still there. And he'd have sworn the dog was smiling at him. That was on Saint Patrick's Day, two, maybe three years ago.

No collar, no tags. Casey wasn't quite full-grown. About nine months, the vet said when Shanahan took him for his shots. Both he and the vet agreed the dog was half hound and half bird dog. The dog's right side was spotted in brown, black, fawn and white. The left was speckled in the same colors. And he could make his eyes real sad, when he wanted to.

"Does he have to come in?" Mrs. Stone looked tired but a little more real. She didn't have time to screw up her face with makeup. "Some of these rugs are worth thousands."

"See, I told you," Shanahan said to the dog; then to the woman, "To the best of my knowledge, Mrs. Stone, Casey hasn't stolen a rug in years."

Mrs. Stone found no humor in Shanahan's remarks. He wondered why she continued to put up with him. He also wondered why he put up with her. He didn't buy the Ouija-board story.

In the entry hall, Mrs. Stone stopped. "So what's next? I've sent Olivia home and I've cleared today's calendar."

"I need a place to set up."

"Set up?"

"A place to sit down, make notes, go through your husband's correspondence, financial records and so forth."

"Is that all necessary?"

"Of course it isn't necessary, unless you want me to try to find your husband."

"You're right. I'm sorry. Couldn't we call a truce or something?"

"I charge eighty-five dollars a day, plus mileage at thirty-five cents a mile and any incidental expenses such as photocopying, parking . . . is that all right?"

"Actually, it's less than . . . yes . . . that will be fine."

So he could have charged more. What was it Rockford charged? Two hundred plus expenses. "I could charge you more if it would give you more confidence."

"That's all right, Mr. Shanahan." She smiled. For a moment he thought he saw a woman who didn't go by Mrs. William B. Stone. Perhaps a Millie or something. "What's his name?" she asked, looking down at the dog.

"Casey."

"Hi, Casey. Can I get him a bowl of water?"

"Maybe later."

The entry hall was large. A wide, cherry-wood stairway went up to a landing, then came back on itself overhead. At the landing, Shanahan noticed a large painting. He recognized the artist from better days, when he and Elaine spent afternoons at local art fairs. The painting was of a male ballet dancer with large, sensitive eyes, done in a wash of watercolors and black ink. A typical Joanie Johnson subject in a typical Joanie Johnson style. Johnson was something of a local celebrity.

To the left of the hallway was the living room. Pleasant, not overdone, but definitely ready for the photographers from *House Beautiful*. The room to the right was richly paneled, with a fireplace, a chesterfield sofa, oriental rugs and a mammoth elaborately carved desk. He thought the desk might be Chinese, but he was hardly an expert in such matters. Behind it, on a narrow table, was a computer, with a printer. All Stone would have to do was swivel his chair and he could play with his expensive electronic toy.

"We can set you up in there if you'd like. It was . . . is Mr. Stone's office. He worked at home."

"A nice house, Mrs. Stone. Did you do it yourself?"

"Heavens, no—this is all Will's doing. His pride and joy."

"You mean he hired the decorators?"

"No, he did it himself. He loved dealing in colors and fabrics."

"I'll bet you picked the painting on the landing."

"Afraid not. That was Will's choice. He always wanted a Joanie."

"Really. Is Mr. Stone a designer? I mean, is that his business?"

"No. Investments, securities—that sort of thing. Wealth management."

"Looks like he managed pretty well," Shanahan said, putting his briefcase, a battered old satchel-like bag that had been through the wars—literally—on the uncluttered desktop.

"He's very respected," she said.

"Bully for him."

"I only say this because I want to explain why I don't want the police involved. At least for now. It may be something silly and I don't want him embarrassed if there's really nothing to worry about, if he's . . ." She stopped, her blank gaze fixed on the wall behind Shanahan.

"We'll have to get into all of that Mrs. Stone."

"I know. May I get you some coffee?"

"Yes, please." His tone softened. He hated liking people he'd already made up his mind to hate. Shanahan preferred the idea of not liking her for another reason. It would be easier to ask the hard questions. Did she and this man, William B. Stone, sleep together? Did Stone have a mistress? Did he have any other personal habits

Shanahan should know about? The questions could wait.
But not for long.

When she left the room, he settled into Stone's chair.
It was comfortable. Mr. Stone must have been about the
same size as Shanahan. He tried to open the middle desk
drawer. Locked. So were the others. He checked the
obvious places for keys. None. Shanahan hunched forward and emptied the contents of his case on the desk: a
small camera, a solar calculator, some powder, a magni-
fying glass, a new spiral notebook and two pens. With one
of them, he wrote on the top of the notebook in all caps:
S-T-O-N-E. Then the date. He repeated the date on the
first page of the notebook.

"Olivia left the coffee on. I don't think it's too old."
Mrs. Stone carried in a silver tray, the cream and sugar
containers in a matched set. "I didn't know how you take
your coffee. Probably black."

"With sugar," he said. "Do you have a key to the
desk?"

"I'm afraid not. One or two teaspoons?"

"Two, at least."

"This was his office. I never meddled."

"Does he have a safe?"

"I don't know, Mr. Shanahan. I know that pretty
much makes me the frivolous housewife. It's what I am. If
he's gone—I mean, for good—then I really have no idea
what to do."

"Weren't you around when they built the house?"

"No. I stayed in our old home as long as I could.
When the buyers moved in, I stayed at my sister's guest
house near Carmel. They have a small farm."

Shanahan could imagine the "farm."

"I'll need to force the lock."

"Is it possible to do it without hurting the wood? It
was . . . is one of Mr. Stone's favorites." Mrs. Stone
stood in the doorway. "Goodness, I almost had him dead,

didn't I? You don't think he's dead do you, Mr. Shana-han?"

Shanahan didn't think Stone was dead. But he did wonder about something. If Stone were having a fling with some floozy, why didn't he just pick up the phone and tell his wife he was out of town? He could have told her anything. If what Mrs. Stone said was true, if she really didn't know anything about hubby's business affairs, then she wouldn't have been savvy enough to question him when he said he was spending a weekend in Philadelphia on business.

Shanahan took prints. Or tried to. Found absolutely nothing on the telephone. What the hell. Did Stone wear gloves? Same thing on the desk. He found only his own set. It took him only seconds to jimmy open the desk drawers. Once the center drawer was open, the other locks disengaged as well. If the desk was an antique, it had been refurbished with a new lock system. Antique desks required the use of a key on each drawer. Inside, there were no personal effects. Just papers, ledgers, and several sets of stationery.

Stone's name appeared on the letterhead of both the state and city chambers of commerce, the Indianapolis 500 Parade Festival Committee, the United Way, and the Pan American Games Committee. There was his own stationery: WILLIAM B. STONE, INC., WEALTH MANAGEMENT. Mrs. Stone was right about not bringing in the police right away. The local business journal would love to get hold of a story about a prominent businessman gone awry. Below the stack of current business stationery, and slightly yellowed, were sheets of stationery that said HUNT, STONE AND KESSLER, INVESTMENT COUNSELORS. What happened to Hunt and Kessler?

———

Shanahan thumbed through the ledgers, noticing the dates stopped way back in 1975. That must have been when he automated his records. Shanahan swiveled, no doubt the way Stone swiveled hundreds of times. Face to face with the computer, Shanahan felt a mild panic.

"I see the present, Casey, and it looks an awful lot like the future to me. What do I know about this shit? I don't even know how to turn the damn thing on." He opened a plastic file next to the computer, gathered the small plastic discs, and put them in his satchel.

Shanahan guessed that Stone's outgoing correspondence was all on the computer file somewhere, but where was the incoming paper? There must be some, but where? He stood up, walked around the office. There had to be a safe somewhere, but even so, not every piece of paper would be in it. Not everything warranted that kind of security.

Knocking on the paneled walls, he discovered a couple of hollow places, then discovered one of them was really a door, flush with the wall but with a small beveled edge. It wasn't an attempt to hide so much as an attempt at subtlety in design. He pulled it open. Inside were shelves with more computer discs and drawers with hanging files. But no safe.

"We're here for the long haul," Shanahan told Casey. The detective took an armful of file folders from the closet and settled in at the desk. One by one, he investigated the files, made notes, going to each new folder with relish. It was a way to bury Elaine, these papers, this obsessive search into another man's life. He was burying her as sure as shoveling dirt into her grave.

What he did notice was the shape of the folders. They were wider at the base than the current contents would have made them. Some stuff had obviously been removed. Recently. Of course that could have been Stone's doing. An orderly guy just sorting through some out-dated, unnecessary papers. Just as the lack of fingerprints could have been the result of Olivia's fine housekeeping skills.

In two hours, he had uncovered little else. Most of it was pretty dry stuff—more financial data, statistics, charts, laboriously written contracts, and letters requesting Stone fund this or that project, attached to fat reports and market surveys. In the older files, Stone uncovered a letter from Kessler. The envelope with a Nicaraguan postmark was still attached. The glue from the envelope caused it to adhere to the back of one of the file folders. It had to do with investments in Managua and San Salvador and Guatamala City. The guy was global—or at least hemispheric.

The shelves also contained checkbooks. Various aligned corporations: WILLIAM B. STONE, INC.; STONE ENTER-PRISES, LTD.; MR. AND MRS. WILLIAM B. STONE. But there were no balances listed. Only blank checks and deposit slips. Stone probably made his entries on the fucking computer. Shanahan ripped out the last deposit slip in each book, went to the entry hall and called out for Mrs. Stone.

She arrived with a tray. Chicken-salad sandwich and potato chips.

He sent her to the banks. Shanahan told her he wanted as much information on each as she could get. Last deposit, last withdrawal, etc. He knew she couldn't get any information on the business accounts, but it would keep her busy for awhile and away from the house.

Next, he let Casey out the front door for a romp. Then he called Harry. For fifty bucks, Harry could find the safe and, with a little luck, open it.

While he waited for Harry, he took a tour of the house, munching on the sandwich. Before he went upstairs, he called Casey back in. Casey put on his sad eyes, hoping for a bite of the sandwich.

"Bad for your teeth. Besides, dogs shouldn't eat mayonnaise," Shanahan said guiltily, greedily. He wondered if Olivia or Mrs. Stone had made it. Casey followed Shanahan upstairs. Both nosed around the closets. The first bedroom had to belong to Mrs. Stone. The bed had been hastily made. Lying across it was a book, *Fine Things*, by Danielle Steel. In the bedside table were two more paperbacks by Steel and a Harlequin Romance.

The bedroom overlooked the front of the house. The room had a dressing area with a well-stocked vanity. Shanahan went into the attached bath and checked the medicine cabinet. It was nearly as well stocked. Dr. Harold Collins's name was on twenty-five or thirty little brown plastic bottles. There were tranquilizers, assorted headache formulas and two bottles of pills with Dilantin in them. He wondered if Mrs. Stone might suffer from epilepsy.

Across the hall was a guest room. So was the room directly next to Mrs. Stone's. Did Olivia stay over? Probably. Something about it suggested use. At the other end was another huge bedroom. The feel of it was similar to the den. Dark, handsome, and meticulous. On the bedside table was a book by Anthony Burgess, *Earthly Powers*. Shanahan sampled a couple of paragraphs in the middle, where the book fell open.

"The guy's a heavyweight, Case. Don't imagine he spends his time watching Cubs games." Shanahan opened the large armoire across from the foot of an ornately carved wood bed. A television and VCR. Curiously, no video cassettes. Shanahan looked back at the bed. It looked as if it belonged to some king named Louis who wouldn't dare go to sleep in his underwear.

The walls of Stone's bath were covered with large black glass tiles. All of the fixtures were white. The floor was black and white marble. Everything so clean, it shined back at you. And his monogrammed towels were white and very thick. The medicine chest, though it contained some pretty pricey male cosmetics, was drug free, unless you counted Excedrin.

The guy didn't leave much of himself out for visitors to see, even nosy ones. Shanahan shooed Casey out of Stone's closet, closed the door, picked up the book by Burgess and took it with him downstairs.

As Shanahan passed through the entry hall, he heard Harry's black van pull up. The muffler was shot, so all the neighbors would know he arrived as well. Casey barked, then jumped on Harry as he came in the door.

"Mixin' with the rich and famous, aren't you, Deets? Down, you ugly beast," he said to Casey. "And you're givin' me fifty? Come now, Deets, after all we've been through."

"She gets the same rates as everybody else. I'm not ripping her off just because she's got money."

"How do you think she got *her* money?"

"I have no idea and it's not my business—or yours. Okay? Just find the safe."

Harry put his metal detector on his shoulder like it was an M1 rifle. "Now, are you sure we're not pulling a job? Looks mighty suspicious." Harry laughed. He knew better.

Shanahan led him into the den.

"The safe has to be in here, but I don't know where. It's not behind the picture."

Harry flicked on the detector and it started ticking right away. "Christ be Jesus," Harry yelled, "either the house is made of steel or we're standing right on it."

Harry moved to the left and the sound died a little. The same when he moved in any other direction. "We're right on it, Deets."

"The rug doesn't come up," Shanahan said. "At least,

not easily. I tried it. Doesn't make any sense to put a safe under a rug nailed to the floor."

"No, it don't." Harry was down on his knees, fingering the carpet, outlining the large pattern in the dead center. He pulled out a knife."

"Hey, that's an expensive rug, Harry. Worth more than I make in a year."

Harry kept going and what Shanahan heard sounded like a mean rip. Harry sat back with a hunk of carpet in his hand, smiling. "Velcro, one of the miracles of modern science."

Harry pulled up a square sheet of planking and pointed at the safe, a few inches below.

"You're beautiful, Harry."

"Will you tell me that *after* we're married, Deets?" Harry kept staring down into the hole.

"What's the matter?"

"The fuckin' thing's electronic, all digital, Deets." Harry looked like someone killed his cat.

"Yeah?"

"Sweetheart, that means ya can't hear the tumblers tumble. This is all new stuff. The kids are into this shit. The only way I know to open something like this is to blow the goddamn thing to kingdom come."

———

Shanahan had other things to think about. Mrs. Stone returned a good hour after Harry left. She hadn't found out anything about the business accounts. The bank wouldn't tell her. And, according to Mrs. Stone, there were no major shifts in funds in or out of their joint account. All seemed normal. He didn't tell Mrs. Stone he had found the safe nor did he tell her much else. He had Maureen on his mind. This evening's date. Fixing dinner. A bottle of wine. And then, well, who knows?

Shanahan did ask Mrs. Stone about Hunt and Kessler

as the two of them stood in the driveway, watching the neighbors' sprinklers spray glistening beads of water on absolutely perfect lawns.

"Bob Hunt was Will's mentor," she said, "brought him into the business and trained him. Will did the same thing for Sam Kessler a few years later when Bob started talking about retirement. When Bob died, Will and Sam decided to split up, go their separate ways."

"How did Hunt die?"

"Cancer, prostate, but he was eighty-three so it came as no great shock."

"Was the split between your husband and Kessler amicable?"

"I don't think it was a horrible thing, but Will and Sam didn't seem to be as close as they once were. I never heard Will speak ill of him."

"Did they see each other after the partnership ended?"

"They could have. But Will never talked about business with me. I do remember a party we had not too many months after Bob died. I was surprised to see Will actually go out of his way to avoid Sam. He doesn't do that kind of thing."

"How did you happen to notice that?"

"Because Sam kept asking me where Will was . . . that he wanted to talk. He laughed and asked if I would help him corner Will. Frankly, I didn't like the look in his eyes, so I told him that I wouldn't join in any plots against my husband, no matter how harmless."

"Did they ever talk?"

"I don't know."

Casey relieved himself against the back tire of the Chevy Malibu, the liquid snaking down the driveway. Mrs. Stone looked but didn't say anything.

"Better there than on the rhododendron," Shanahan said.

———

Since he was already on this side of town, he could stop by O'Malia's food market on his way back and pick up some chicken breasts, some fresh asparagus and a decent wine. Would he know a decent wine if he saw one? He wasn't sure, but the market had little cards by the wine racks that would help.

At home, he soaked the chicken in a bottle of Kraft Fiesta Salad Dressing—Craig Claiborne, he wasn't—then covered the dish with a plate so the cat wouldn't be tempted. More than once, Einstein had made off with the main course. Even now, the thief sat a couple of feet away, studying the loot and calculating the angles of attack and escape.

He put in a call to Harry. No answer. He called the bar.

"You're one helluva detective, Deets. Tracked me right down," Harry said. "But Sherlock, you've interrupted a profound treatise on why dogs have assholes."

"Harry, I need to find somebody who knows something about computers."

"See, there was this big dog convention. Every dog in the entire world came—"

"Harry, listen, could we make this quick?" If Shanahan couldn't stop him, then maybe he could hurry him up.

"Well, when they got there, the sergeant at arms asked each dog to check his asshole at the door and the poodle in the checkroom gave them each a number."

"Yeah, yeah, I get the picture." This wasn't going to be one of Harry's good stories. There was probably a crowd at the bar and he was warming them up, a setup for one of his epics.

"Right in the middle of the big meeting, a fire broke out. Now this put them all in a panic and they were in such a hurry to leave, they just grabbed the first asshole they could find and got the hell out of there. Ever since, they've been sniffing each other out, trying to find their own." Shanahan could hear the laughter in the background. Harry would drink free the rest of the night.

"Well?" Harry said, "You're not laughing."

"I heard it in '59."

"You did not."

"Do you know anybody who knows anything about computers?"

"How would I know anybody who knows computers? I can't even get my card back from those damn bank machines."

"Think, Harry."

"I'm thinking, I'm thinking. Shit. Zilch. Oh shit, wait a minute. My grandkid's boyfriend. He's crazy 'bout that kinda crap."

"How can I get hold of him?"

"How do I know, Deets?" Harry sounded perturbed. "Yeah, well now that you've stopped the act cold, I could take a minute and call Jasmine."

"Your granddaughter?"

"No, my wife."

"I thought Ruth was your wife."

"Ruth *was* my wife. Helen *was* my wife. What's-her-name *was* my wife, for Christ's sake. And so was Jasmine."

"Sorry, Harry. It's just that every time you told a wife story you just talked about Ruth." You know a guy and, then again, you don't.

"Easier that way. I just sorta rolled up all the stories into one wife, so I wouldn't have to do all that explainin'. Anyway, Jasmine was the wife that had the kid. If she's feelin' a little melancholy, she'll be glad to help. She'll call the kid and the kid will call her boyfriend and her boyfriend will call you and you can set up the meeting."

"What if Jasmine isn't feeling a little melancholy?"

"Then, she'll tell me to put my butt in the oven and I'll tell you to put your butt in the oven and our gooses will be cooked."

"Can you start this little telephone game right away?"

"Why the hell not? I've already lost my audience."

"Thanks, Harry."

"Don't mention it. Just laugh when I tell you a funny story for Christ's sake. Don't cost nothing to laugh."

———

Shanahan found himself staring down at the asparagus. What was he supposed to do with them? Boil them? Steam them? Wasn't he supposed to cut off the ends? He opened his refrigerator and looked into the freezer compartment. Buried in the glaciers of ice was a package of frozen peas. His insurance policy in the event he wrecked the asparagus.

"No insurance policies, Casey?" Shanahan said suddenly remembering their absence. They had to be in the safe or a safety deposit box. Casey put on his sad eyes, unrequited longing for something off the kitchen counter. "Asparagus, kid," Shanahan said, handing him a spear. Casey sniffed, then looked at Shanahan like he'd been offered a wet sponge. "Sorry, you like potatoes. How was I to know?" Casey left.

Maureen was due at eight. He was nervous. She was a puzzle. Everything was a puzzle. Mrs. Stone and her Ouija board. The very neat Mr. Stone. The missing insurance policies. The goddamn safe? Stone's computer sitting there impregnable, at least to a man who just got used to electronic calculators instead of adding machines. Then, there was his son. Ty was willing to fly out and meet his maker, at least until Dad screwed it up. Shanahan didn't even know how to contact him. Then again, what would he do if he found him?

Shanahan dried his hands and went into the living room. Was it presentable? It would have to be. He went into the bedroom, smoothed out the bedspread, and threw his reading glasses, his keys and his change into the top bureau drawer. The room—the house—still had Elaine's stamp on it, and it made him feel like he was cheating on her. If Maureen stayed the night . . . well, would she? Was it even a possibility? Was she just being nice to someone who reminded her of her own father? Just someone safe. Or whether . . . what? What? He didn't know.

She wasn't innocent, that was for damned sure. He met her "professionally" at the Adult Relaxation Center. What would Elaine have thought? What would Ty think if he knew? Well, it wasn't the first time. Shanahan wasn't a monk. And it was only a massage. Could have been more, maybe, but it wasn't. She was nice, easy to be with. Someone who seemed to listen even when you weren't talking. So who cares what anybody thinks.

She was a nice woman. What in the hell was he talking about? He had known her for precisely one hour last week. He had been nervous, as he always was when he went to these places. The old converted house on West Washington Street, with the closed-in front porch. They all looked alike. Privacy fence around the parking lot so nobody would recognize a car or see you coming and going. The paneling inside, straight from Central Hardware. Girls asleep on cheap sofas.

The woman at the desk lines the customer up with Maureen and they hit it off. He invites her to dinner. She accepts.

3

A half a glass of J. W. Dant with two ice cubes settled him down a bit. Maureen arrived after the third sip, carrying two bottles of wine. One red. One white.

"Didn't know what you were cooking," she said. Crossing the room, she kissed him quickly on the cheek and headed toward the kitchen as if she'd lived there all her life. He heard the refrigerator open and close, and she was back, sighed, looked squarely in his eyes. "Smells good."

"Me or the kitchen?"

"Do I look all right?" She knew she did.

A loose white blouse, a couple of buttons open and high-waisted khaki slacks that fell loosely after the fabric passed her hips.

"Fine." Shanahan was nervous again. She was prettier than he remembered. Auburn hair, green eyes. She looked younger, too, but anyone would look younger out of the harsh light of the stark white room and the green-tinted fluorescence of the massage parlor. Her lips weren't quite so red and she had let up a bit on the makeup.

"Would you mind fixing me a drink?" She smiled, forward, playful.

He went to the kitchen to double-check his liquor supply. "I have bourbon, rum, and vodka. I have coke, club soda, and tonic water. Your pleasure?" he called out.

She was standing in the doorway. "Rum, tonic and a twist of lemon if you have it."

He did. He had bought lemon for the chicken.

"What do I call you, anyway? Shanahan? That's what you wrote down. Just Shanahan."

"You've got my last name and I have your first. That's a great way to start an intimate dinner, don't you think?" Shanahan said.

"Suits me. My last name is Smith."

"Right."

"No, it is. For God's sake there are a million Smiths in the world, real ones, somebody has to have that last name." She went to the living room and brought back her purse, dumping it out on the counter.

"Here," she said, handing him her driver's license.

"Maureen D. Smith, 2035 North Drexel . . ." he read out loud. "Age? Let's see, that'd make you forty-three."

"Not until December." She looked at him, one eyebrow raised. "Well?"

"Well?"

"What are you? Like Liberace, only have one name?"

"It's Dietrich. Some people call me Deets."

"What do the others call you?"

"Shanahan."

"All right, Shanahan it is. I like that best."

———

After dinner, she disappeared. Shanahan came out of the kitchen and called to her. No answer. He checked the bedrooms, and eventually found her out in the backyard. She was stretched out on the grass under the ancient sycamore. Casey was laying beside her.

"It's really nice, Shanahan," Maureen said gesturing toward the yard and garden. "You must have two hundred lilies over there."

"They'll start blooming in June."

"Will you invite me back to see them?"

Shanahan came over and sat down. "Sure. Open invitation."

"What do you believe in, Shanahan?"

Jesus, she changed subjects quickly. "What do you mean? God? A supreme master of the universe?"

"That sort of thing. Anything really. What do you believe in?"

Shanahan was quiet for a long time. She waited.

"This," he said.

"You mean the garden, the flowers."

"Yeah."

"The sky, trees, rain, that stuff?"

"Yeah."

"Yeah?" She was challenging him on something. He didn't quite know what.

"Yeah. I guess. I don't know what you're driving at."

"You don't believe in things man-made."

"I guess not. Why?" Shanahan said. "What point are you trying to make?"

"No point. Just trying to know you. You don't reveal too much." She looked away, then casually, "You got burnt once, didn't you?"

"Come on. No amateur psychiatry. Everybody gets burnt."

"Nature's not always kind, either. I mean a cat gets the bird. Some squirrel comes along and eats the roots of your fern."

"But nature's not premeditated. It is what it is. It doesn't beat around the bush, so to speak."

She smiled. "I deserved that. But humor me just a minute more. I want to know what you're sure of, what you believe in for sure. Without a doubt. You sure the sun's going to rise tomorrow?"

"The odds are in favor of it."

"And if the weatherman says sunrise is at six-fifteen, you going to stand there with a watch to make sure?"

"Who cares what the weatherman says? I'm sure that we're going to have night and day. And that's about all I'm sure of. Then, one day, one of two things happen. Either the sun doesn't rise and then nothing matters, or one day I don't rise and then nothing matters."

"And meanwhile?" she asked, getting comfortable, putting her hand on his thigh.

"Meanwhile, some things matter."

"You have cable?" she asked suddenly sitting up.

"Yes." Shanahan had to smile.

"First time I've seen you do that."

"Hope you have a photographic memory," Shanahan said drily.

"We can catch the last few innings of the Cubs game."

Shanahan smiled and shook his head.

"That's twice," she reminded him.

"You're a lucky girl."

"Can I stay the night?"

"Yeah." It was an effort to keep up with her.

"Ten to one, Williams is pitching right now, trying to save the game."

Shanahan got up. She held out her hands and he pulled her up off the grass. They headed back to the house. "I'd have thought you wanted to watch Ryne Sandburg," Shanahan said. "His face was made for the front of a Wheaties box."

Maureen laughed. "That's true. A hunk. He'll be a real looker in about thirty years when he gets a little character in his face."

She looked up and caught another grin. "That's three times. I consider it an honor."

———

Shanahan hated telephones. Days interrupted by insurance salesmen pushing Medicare supplements. How many times had he rushed out of the shower to talk to a computer? Or to listen to some canned sales pitch that told him how lucky he was to have been chosen to receive something free, that of course wasn't free at all? Aluminum siding, magazines, a book of coupons?

Now he was being dragged from a pleasant sleep. Half awake, he prayed the ringing would stop. He was so comfortable, warm, relaxed. Shanahan glanced at the clock. Nine-thirteen said the blue-green numbers. He never slept that late. He discovered, also to his surprise, that he was in bed, not on the sofa where he usually ended up sleeping. When he shifted in bed to answer the phone, his foot touched another warm body. For Christ's sake, he wasn't alone.

He remembered who it was with the auburn hair asleep beside him and why it was.

"Shanahan," he said into the phone, his voice an octave deeper than it would be later in the day.

"This is Harmony McCord," said the voice on the other end. The voice was male, young, clear and unfamiliar.

"So?" Shanahan said, poised to lay into a home improvement salesman with a stupid name.

"Harry said you were looking for someone to help you with computer records."

"Oh yes, I'm sorry."

Maureen moved beside him, whispering a good morning. He saw the faint freckles covering her shoulders. She was as attractive as she was last night. Maybe more so. A certain vulnerability . . .

"What is it I can help you with?" the voice belonging to Harmony McCord asked.

"I have some plastic discs from a computer. I need to know what's on them."

"What kind of computer?"

"A small one."

Harmony laughed. "Do you know if it's an IBM or an Apple? A personal computer, probably, a PC?"

"Probably. I don't know much about these things. I

didn't get the brand, but it's whitish and has a little screen and a printer and there was a white box next to it, connected to the screen."

"Why don't you drop the discs by this morning, if you want. I can take a look. We'll figure it out."

"I'd appreciate it. Will it take long?"

"I don't know yet. I'll know when I see them."

Harmony gave him the address. They were to meet at ten-thirty.

Maureen had slipped on her blouse and was in the bathroom. Shanahan could hear the water running. Seemed strange having someone in the house. It seemed strange to wake up at nine. He was usually up by six. Einstein was on the bed, meowing. It was past his feeding time and he knew the cat wouldn't shut up until he had a plate full of 9-Live's veal slices and gravy.

———

Casey had fallen asleep in the backseat by the time Shanahan picked up the interstate that led him just north of the heart of downtown. The Indianapolis 500 banners were up on the light poles. The temporary bleachers were in place for the big parade. He had forgotten this was the big month. The big year, actually. The PGA was already scheduled. People were talking Super Bowl and Olympics. The "Naptown" Shanahan had known was waking up. Huge cranes hovered over new construction throughout the downtown.

Harmony lived or worked in Fountain Square, just south of The Circle, two miles or so. Gentrification was only hinted at there, a tough white neighborhood with its own little downtown. Used bookstores, second-hand stores, a genuine Woolworth's and empty theater buildings.

The address was just off the main intersection. Parking wasn't difficult because nobody went there anymore.

He entered what was an old factory or warehouse, climbed some rickety stairs and knocked on the door with the hand-lettered sign that said Graphikworks.

Shanahan expected to find some kid with black-rimmed glasses, the kind who used to walk around with a slide rule sticking out of his back pocket in high school. Trigonometry freaks. What he found was quite different.

The kid at the door had long dark hair, wore a Hawaiian-print shirt, jeans and sneakers. His demeanor was casual, open. Shanahan was about to ask if it was okay for Casey to come in, but Harmony laid all fears to rest by dropping on his haunches, looking directly at Casey.

"Hi, fella." Harmony scratched Casey's ear. "You're a fine dog."

There was a bark from the far end of the room and in moments a golden retriever was making its way toward them.

"Diana, meet . . ."

"Casey," Shanahan said.

"Casey," Harmony repeated. After a moment of investigation, which reminded Shanahan of Harry's dog convention story, Casey barked, dropped down on his front paws with his rear end up in the air and barked again. Diana, the dog, did the same.

"This could be love," Harmony said.

Shanahan glanced around the room. It went on for miles. The refinished wooden-plank floors reflected the light from a row of big factory-style windows.

"Let me show you around my office," Harmony said, leading Shanahan to a computer setup, the likes of which Shanahan couldn't have imagined. It looked like the set of a futuristic movie. There were at least three small computers, one of which looked similar to Stone's. There were two TV monitors, a video camera, a still camera on a tripod, several strange-looking electronic devices, keyboards and something that looked like an electronic piano.

Shanahan couldn't imagine how a kid, well on the light side of thirty, could afford all this kind of computer getup.

"What kind of work do you do?" Shanahan asked.

"All kinds. I help set up computer systems, mostly graphic work. I take in business doing charts, graphs, maps for annual reports. In fact that's about a third of my business. Another third is the work I do for plastic and reconstructive surgeons." Harmony sat down in front of what appeared to be the central work station. "Now, let me see what you have here."

Shanahan handed him a bag full of plastic discs. "I don't know what's on them."

"We'll find out," Harmony said confidently, but without arrogance. "Whose are these?"

"Some guy's," Shanahan said coldly.

"Harry said you were a private investigator. I just want to know two things. Is what I'm doing legal? And second, more important, knowing what kind of work this person does will help me figure out what kind of system he uses."

"I'm sorry. Yes, it's legal. And the guy's into some kind of financial business."

"Well, then, chances are he's using IBM or COMPAQ. An IBM II, I'd guess from the discs. I don't have either."

"Does that mean you can't help?"

"No, it means I'll probably have to play around with it for a little while. I can probably tell you something by tonight and get whatever you want by tomorrow evening. If you want print outs it might take an extra day. There's a lot of stuff here."

"Cost?"

"You're a friend of Harry's."

"No, this is business. But I'll need to have a rough idea so I can tell my client about the expense."

"Well, I can't tell you much until I take a look. Could be as little as fifty or as much as two-fifty."

"No problem," Shanahan said. "What do you do for plastic surgeons?"

"Alter faces," Harmony said.

Shanahan must have looked puzzled. "Sounds criminal."

"Sit down over there," Harmony told him.

Shanahan sat in the chair facing the video camera. Above the camera was a TV screen. When Harmony flipped a switch, some lights came on, illuminating Shanahan. Another switch and Shanahan could see himself on TV. Harmony sat down in front of a computer screen and in moments Shanahan's image from the TV monitor appeared on the screen.

"Now, scoot up here by me," Harmony said.

Shanahan's face was frozen on the computer screen. "Now I can do anything I want with you. I can make your nose larger." Harmony used a pencil-type stick connected to a wire. He extended the nose. Shanahan as Pinocchio.

"Or, I can put it back the way it was." Harmony pushed a button and Shanahan was Shanahan again. "People who want or need plastic surgery can get an idea of what they will look like after the operation. Or they can use this to design their own new faces." Harmony leaned back in his chair, then suddenly lurched forward. "I have an idea. Let's see what you looked like a few years ago."

While Shanahan watched, Harmony erased wrinkles, pulled in the flesh under Shanahan's chin, firmed up the skin, made his hair dark, even lowered Shanahan's hairline an inch or so.

Shanahan just then became aware of the music and Harmony seemed to sense it. "Brian Eno."

"What?" Shanahan asked, a little startled.

"Brian Eno. The music. It's a lot like Muzak . . . only different. All electronic."

"Oh," Shanahan said, entranced by the young Shanahan emerging on the screen.

"You look like somebody," Harmony said, looking back and forth from the screen to the real-life Shanahan.

"I am somebody." Casey and the dog Diana were lying side by side in a patch of sunlight. The oddly colored mongrel and the full-blooded golden retriever.

Harmony leaned back in his chair. He was tan, clear-eyed and very much at home with himself. "No, I mean a movie star or something. It's familiar. I don't know where from."

"What else can you do with this thing?"

"Well, we can take a photograph or an image from videotape and manipulate it any way we want. We can take things out of the picture and nobody could tell they were ever there. Or we can put things in."

"Nobody could tell, not even experts?"

"No. It's all done with pixels, dots. Experts can suspect, knowing the capability of such computer manipulation, but they can't prove it."

"So photographs shouldn't be used in courts?"

"They're certainly becoming less reliable pieces of evidence, but the technology is so new, not very many people know about it."

"So, you're dating Harry's granddaughter?" Shanahan said, trying not to think about how different the future would be and how fast it moved by him.

"Yeah, we're talking marriage." Harmony shook his head. "Only talking. She's a little scared. So am I. It's scary."

Shanahan thought the computers were pretty scary, but didn't say so.

———

It was almost one-thirty when Shanahan arrived at the Stone residence. Mrs. Stone ushered Shanahan and Casey to the sun deck, off the kitchen. It overlooked the reservoir. A long lawn sloped down toward the water. The light was almost blinding, but looking through the trees— some of them had been there long before the house was built—Shanahan could make out twenty or thirty sailboats in the distance, floating on the shiny surface. Casey immediately took the opportunity to stretch his legs and declare the land his by annointing each tree.

"I'm afraid I have to know some things, Mrs. Stone. It might get uncomfortable for you," Harry said, sitting down at the umbrella table. Olivia, a vibrant, slim young black woman brought out a tray with watermelon, canta- loupe, and strawberries, some cheese and cold sliced turkey. Her quick glance at Shanahan, however, wasn't friendly.

"I know," Mrs. Stone said, indicating that while it was unpleasant, she would do her best. Each time he saw her, she seemed more relaxed.

"I don't mean to make you angry, but you seem to be taking this pretty well."

"It's very strange, Mr. Shanahan," Mrs. Stone said, picking up a strawberry, then putting it down. "I feel better. If I have any anxiety at all, I'm afraid it's the possibility he'll come back."

Shanahan started to ask a question, but was cut off.

"I think I can answer all your questions without your having to ask them. We married young, Will and I. Even before he got out of Harvard. We had the support of our parents, the encouragement really. Pressure perhaps." She nodded, as if it was the first time she understood. "We never . . . ah . . . never . . . became lovers, Mr. Shanahan."

Shanahan was distracted. He could hear Casey barking, but couldn't see him.

"We never argued. We liked each other a great deal. We respected each other. I was there for him socially. He was there for me. He kept my life in order. Look"—she gestured back up to the big house—"how could I complain? I couldn't manage something like that. I can't manage my own financial affairs. I didn't."

"Is it true what you said about finding me with a Ouija board?"

Casey was barking louder. Shanahan stood up and yelled for him, but Casey didn't come. Then he saw him emerge from beneath a giant blue spruce, the kind with boughs that droop all the way down to the ground. Casey barked like a hunting dog who had treed his prey.

"No possum hunting, Case. Let go of whatever you have in there."

Casey whined, yelped, then barked, using every sound he could create to let Shanahan know it was important. Shanahan knew there was something seriously wrong.

Casey had different barks for different things. A standard bark was used to announce the mailman and other unknown visitors. Same one for cats. He growled, deep, low, and deadly at possums. He yelped when he was frustrated, when Shanahan teased him with a Milk-Bone or refused to throw the ball.

Casey had something serious to show Shanahan and he wouldn't budge. And he wouldn't shut up.

"I'll have to go see," he told Mrs. Stone. The early afternoon shadows were already harsh. The air was still. All was absolutely quiet in the world. Too quiet. Shanahan sensed something ominous in the long trek toward the blue spruce. He could feel the hair rising on his neck. He knew what he was going to find.

Shanahan swept back the branch, feeling each sharp needle on the back of his hand. Casey had uncovered a corpse. There in the shade, a man's head and an arm stuck out of the ground as if the lifeless body had died while trying to crawl out.

4

Olivia had taken Mrs. Stone inside, not before she had given Shanahan a good long glare, however. She had instructions to call the doctor. Shanahan felt foolish standing by the tree waiting for the police to arrive. Why? The corpse wasn't going anywhere.

The police car got there. A few minutes later, Dr. Collins arrived. Collins went inside and Shanahan stood out back, talking with one of the two policemen.

"You her dad or somethin'?" asked the older and heavier of the two. The other cop was still looking at the body.

"Something."

"Look fella—"

"The name is Shanahan." He relented. He was making trouble for himself. "I was hired by Mrs. Stone."

"To do what?"

"To find Mr. Stone."

The younger cop came over. "Looks like you found him. You're a P.I. then?"

"That's right."

Shanahan reached down to pat Casey, calm him down. The dog wasn't fond of uniforms.

"Then, let's see your license, pops," said the older cop.

"He ain't a pops, dickhead." It was a familiar voice, but Shanahan didn't recognize the face that went with it. A big man, three-piece suit despite the heat, a beard, about fifty. "Good afternoon, Shanahan," the man said; then to the uniformed policemen, "Why don't you two goofballs see if the coroner is on his way and make sure Hans brings the camera. Comprendez?"

"Right, Max," said the younger cop.

"Right, Max," said the older cop, mimicking as the two went back around to the front of the house.

"Max Rafferty," Shanahan said, "I didn't recognize you without your scooter."

"In all his glorious if not ponderous flesh. How're you doing Shanahan? I figured you'd have a fishing pole out in the Florida gulf by now. How's Elaine?"

"Dead," Shanahan said. He resented having to think about her. He also thought he remembered not liking Rafferty. Not sure why. It was a long time ago.

"That kinda thing has been going around lately."

"You look like you won the lottery, Max."

"Oh, this." Rafferty ran his hands down the lapels of his expensive suit. "You're no doubt referring to my sartorial splendor. Well, my friend, I'm a lieutenant now. Where's the late Mr. Stone?"

Shanahan pulled back the branches of the spruce.

"Looks like a suicide to me," Rafferty said, smiling.

"Yeah, the guy dug a hole, shot himself in the head, then covered himself up. Neat guy."

"Hey, don't laugh. Not too long ago, there was a guy in—what's the name of that burg? Well anyway, twenty-two hammer blows to the head and the local constabulary rules it self-inflicted. Determined little fucker. Where's the lady of the mansion?"

"Inside with the doctor and the housekeeper."

"She I.D. him?"

"No, but it's Stone."

"You were hired to do what? Find the gent?"

"Yeah."

"How long was he missing?"

"Four, five days. He didn't come back on Friday

night. I talked to her on Monday, took the job on Tuesday."

"Found him on Wednesday. You're good, Shanahan. Why didn't she call us?"

"I think she thought he might be having an affair. Didn't want the papers in on it."

"He do that kind of thing?"

"No. Not so far as I know," Shanahan said.

"Well, the papers gonna be on it like it was a presidential assassination. Chief called me personally. The mayor's concerned. He wants to be governor. The prosecutor's licking his chops because he wants to be mayor. Stone's big behind the scenes. You know, what gets built in this city, state maybe, and what doesn't. Big-time Republican, part of the king-making machine. How many Democratic senators, mayors we have in the past thirty years? One fluke governor, that's it. Otherwise, zero." Rafferty looked at Shanahan's bored expression. "Am I telling you things you didn't know?"

Shanahan walked back up to the deck and sampled a piece of cheese. He knew what Rafferty wanted.

"Come on, Shanahan. Your turn. Talk to me," Rafferty said.

"I was hired to find him. He's found. Not my case anymore."

Rafferty followed. "You tell her that?"

"Not yet."

"Maybe she'll want to keep you on."

"Wouldn't know why. Everything's going to be blown open. And you said yourself this is a priority case with you guys."

"That's why we have to talk. I don't put the pieces together and quick, I'll be back riding a three-wheeler in parades and wearing polyester suits. Look, let me get the coroner started and I'll meet you at René's in Broad Ripple. About an hour. They have the best potato salad in the world, chocolate cheesecake that's better than sex. My treat."

"I don't know anything, Rafferty, at least not anything Mrs. Stone can't tell you in five minutes." Shanahan knew he wasn't going to cooperate with Rafferty and he wasn't sure why. Maybe it was the expensive suit. Life looked pretty easy for Rafferty.

"Shanahan, we always got along all right, didn't we?" Rafferty was patronizing. "I didn't treat you like a P.I. schnook. So, let's do it nice. If I take you downtown, we sit for hours drinking lousy coffee out of paper cups. Then I get all cranky and I don't like me and I don't like you. René's is a nice little place. It's after the rush. We take a little walk along the canal. Feed the ducks."

"We could hold hands and talk about our future together."

Rafferty laughed. "Now you're talking, Shanahan. We all need a little romance in our lives." Rafferty looked up behind Shanahan. "Hey, you goofballs!" Rafferty yelled at the two cops coming back around the house, followed by a scrawny little man clutching a camera. "Where's the goddamn coroner?"

Shanahan took one final walk around the grounds, then went back through the house to say good-bye to Mrs. Stone. He changed his mind when he saw Rafferty engaged in what appeared to be an intimate conversation with Olivia. But then, that was Rafferty's way. He was more like a P.R. man—the slimy type—than a cop. When he wanted something, he was your best friend. When he didn't, he couldn't remember your name.

———

"So I get ribbed. Little Caesar, you know, our beloved prosecutor, says I look like a pervert and the chief says I look like a communist," said Rafferty, taking his first bite of the cheesecake. "I says the beard's gotta stay cause I got a skin condition. I can get a doctor to tell you I gotta skin condition."

"Is it true?"

"Course it's true. Everybody's got a skin condition. I ask the doctor the condition of my skin. He says 'good.' So I have a good skin condition. It's a condition, isn't it? I wanted a beard all my life. Now looking like I do, two hundred and eighty pounds, I gotta do something that makes me look distinguished. Makes me look like the guy in the movies. What's his name? *Citizen Kane*. Orson Welles, that's the guy. Now, I'd rather look like Rock Hudson or somebody. Maybe not Hudson, but Cary Grant or somebody, but I'm never going to look like that. Now, it's surprising. I get more respect. Some women actually find me attractive. Never did before. And, there's a side benefit. I scare the shit out of people. They don't know there's a little wimp inside."

Rafferty took a deep breath and pushed half a piece of cheesecake toward the middle of the table. "Now, the coroner guesses it was late Thursday night when Stone meets the grim reaper. Bullet through the head, close range. Three feet maybe. The bullet goes in, but it don't come out. So, it's probably small caliber. All guesses for now, but doc's pretty good, won't have missed it by much."

Rafferty took another bite, shoved the plate toward Shanahan, offering him a bite. "This shit is good," Rafferty said.

Shanahan shook his head and Rafferty pulled the plate back to him, took another bite and tried to talk. "Anyways, Stone's wearing nothing but a towel. Probably shot in his own backyard. What do you think—the guy's getting ready for bed, hears something, goes out back, runs into a burglar?"

"Could be," Shanahan said. The waiter came over, started to take Rafferty's half-eaten cheesecake.

"Whoa, fellow," Rafferty said, brandishing a fork. "I'm just resting." Then he leaned across the table to Shanahan. "A burglar don't shoot somebody that close. He don't take the time to bury the body. Sounds to me like the guy—or is it a guy?—knows Stone. What do you think?"

"I think you're way ahead of me. I think I don't know any more than you do."

Rafferty shoved himself back from the table. "What? A chicken-salad sandwich ain't enough? You want a steak or something before you fill me in on the details?"

"There wasn't any reason for me to believe he had been murdered before I found the body." Shanahan chose his words carefully.

"The corpse kinda clued you in, huh?" Rafferty smirked, then shook his head. "Good, Shanahan. You're doin' real good."

"In fact, I didn't find much of anything. Stone didn't believe in laying anything around that might reveal his character. All I know is that he read thick books with a lot of big words, liked art and had a pretty unemotional relationship with his wife." There, that was enough to pay for his sandwich.

"You know"—Rafferty reached across the table, fork in hand, and took another bite of the cheesecake, savoring the taste—"funniest thing, the guy's got this computer and he don 't have anything to put in it."

There was a long silence. Rafferty raised one eyebrow—an all-knowing look—and again showed his irksome smile. Shanahan remembered the attitude and confirmed his reasons for not liking Rafferty.

"I've got them, the discs. I'm having them analyzed. Nothing but business records, probably."

"Probably. But you shouldn't be taking evidence. That's a criminal offense."

"At the time I took them, there wasn't a crime. Nobody knew he was dead."

"Somebody did, but I get your point. You'll have to return them, and it'd be real nice of you if you shared your analysis. What about insurance policies? Wills?"

"Can't find them."

"The guy have a safe?"

"Did you find one?" Shanahan asked.

"No. Did you?"

"Now, if you and your boys can't find a safe, how could a half-retired P.I.?"

———

When Shanahan got home, there was a note pinned to his door:

> I didn't get a chance to thank you for dinner. If you've got nothing better to do, I'd like to return the favor tonight. Your place? I fix a mean monkfish. Call me.

She signed it "The pushy broad," and left a phone number.

———

Einstein was using his mournful cry routine to get Shanahan to fix his evening meal. It irritated Shanahan and it irritated Casey, who chased the feline onto the kitchen counter. Einstein reached down and gave the dog a wicked left jab.

The phone rang. Shanahan grabbed the wall phone, using his shoulder to hold it to his ear while he continued to dip out a half can of 9-Lives Tender Veal and Cheese dinner.

"Where have you been? I've been trying to find you for two hours."

It was Mrs. Stone. She was bereaved. She was pissed. Einstein was nudging Shanahan's hand, encouraging him to hurry with the grub.

"I'm sorry, Mrs. Stone. You were upstairs with the doctor. I didn't think you would want to be bothered with me right then."

She softened. "You're the only person I can talk to—aside from my sister. And I really can't talk to her about all of this. She's not all that well and . . ."

"There's not that much I can do right now, Mrs. Stone. The police—"

"You can find out who did it," she said, angry again.

"That's what I'm trying to say. The police are going to give this case top priority, put all their resources to work on it. Your husband was important, politically. I'd just be taking your money."

"Money is not an object, Mr. Shanahan," she said sternly, then after a pause she said very quietly, "You make me feel calm. I don't know where all of this leads. Just stay by me for a while at least. The police. The reporters. I'm not used to all this."

Shanahan agreed to stay on. The cat ate his food as if he hadn't been fed in a month. Shanahan looked at the note and decided to call Maureen. He didn't know what he was going to say. He called her anyway.

It was the receptionist at the Adult Relaxation Center who answered the phone. He was sorry he called, but he had already given his name. "I'll see if she's busy," the lady said.

He waited too long. He had time to picture the place and to picture Maureen practicing her profession.

"Thanks for calling, Shanahan." Her voice was warm.

"Yeah, well . . . it's probably not good for me to call you at work. You might be with somebody." Christ, he said stupid things.

"Well, actually I am, but he'll hold for a minute or two."

Shanahan felt a stab of jealousy. It was a feeling, one he hadn't felt in years, decades maybe. But it was familiar. It was like he'd been hit in the stomach, below the belt.

"Look, I'll call you later." He tried to disguise his anger. He couldn't. His voice was ice.

"Sure. I have to get back to this hunk. You know the type, wavy black hair, muscles to die for."

Shanahan hung up. He stood there staring at the phone. It rang.

"Shanahan, the guy weighs ninety-eight pounds. No hair. Nice guy, but a little squirrely. What he's getting is a massage, just like you. Not all the girls here go the extra mile, do you know what I mean? If this guy wants something more, then I move him on to somebody who'll give him what he wants. So, if you don't feel like a fool yet, you might think about it until you do."

Shanahan was quiet.

"Do you feel like a fool yet?" she asked.

He did, but he couldn't formulate the words.

"I'll be over at seven," she said, "unless you don't want me to."

"Maureen . . . I . . . ah . . . look . . ."

"If all of this is too complicated, it's okay," Maureen said calmly. "I'd really like to see you again, but I'll understand if you don't. It's better to put an end to this now, if it's not what you want. I could deal with that. Chalk it up to one great evening. I'll settle for that. Later, it might not be so easy and I don't believe in suffering, Shanahan. I believe in happiness. Now, I've got to get back. The poor guy's probably freezing his ass off, what little he has."

"You want me to toss a salad?" Shanahan asked.

5

What Shanahan told himself was that he needed to drop by the grocery and get some cat food. He didn't believe it for a minute. He knew he wanted a beer. Or two. And he didn't feel like drinking alone. He had an hour, maybe more, before Maureen arrived.

Delaney had a beer on the counter even before Shanahan reached the stool. Harry wasn't there. The big-screen TV magnified a blond guy in a blue suit talking about the Middle East. And it reminded Shanahan of Kessler.

"It's like a morgue in here, Delaney."

"Yeah, well it gets that way sometimes. Gives me a chance to bone up on current affairs. And that's what we got. Current affairs. HUD. The PTL. You think he's queer?"

"Who?"

"The preacher. They say he made eyes at some guy."

"How do you do that?" Shanahan asked.

"Do what?"

"Make eyes."

"Hell, I don't know, I'm not a pansy," Delaney said. "Like this, maybe?" Delaney put his hands on his hips, pursed his lips, made his eyes real big. He was getting into it.

Then came a great booming voice from a guy a few feet inside the door. "So that's what two Irishmen do when nobody else is around?"

"Gamble?" Shanahan said, recognizing him. "What is this, a vice raid? Haven't seen you in years."

"Ought to be a raid," Gamble said, pointing to an

embarrassed Delaney. "You'd get twenty years to life just for being so ugly."

"I was pretending to be that preacher guy. What's his name? Tammy's husband? Bakker. Jim Bakker."

"Don't matter to me. I'm off duty." Gamble pulled up a stool next to Shanahan. "How the hell you been, boy? Been looking through the obits and you were a no show, so I thought you must have croaked in Saint Pete or someplace."

"Could have found me here most of the time," Shanahan said. "I'd have my wake here if it weren't for Delaney selling the place out from under me. I wanted to be stood up over there in the corner by the jukebox."

"No! Selling out are you, Delaney? What? You going downtown? Everybody else is. Shit, a few years ago, everybody was flocking to get out of downtown. Now . . . well, hell . . . there must be thirty new bars opened up down there in the last couple of years."

"Getting out," Delaney said. "Figure I put in my time."

"Know what you mean. You still working, Shanahan?"

"Retired for the most part."

"But still take a case now and then, I bet. Keep your hand in?"

Gamble pulled out his trademark rum-soaked crook cigar. Other than getting older and even more unkempt, Gamble looked pretty much the same. Ashes on the lapel of his frayed jacket. Tie too short to reach across a big belly. Teeth turned green, or brown, from the cigars.

"Remember our euchre nights, Shanahan?"

"Yeah."

"We'd be dealing the cards and Elaine would be running through the room like a banshee, armed with a Lysol can, spraying the cigar smoke."

"I remember."

"Finally, she got so cranky we started meeting here. That's how we found this place, remember?"

"Yeah."

"Shit," Gamble said, "whatever happened to our game?"

"Wives. Kids," Shanahan said. "Some people just stopped showing up."

"Guess that means me, doesn't it?" Gamble looked a little sheepish.

"Didn't mean anything by it," Shanahan said. "I understand."

"Hell, Delaney was afraid the cops would come in, break up the game. Did no good to remind him I'm a cop. I even worked vice then."

"What are you doing now?" Shanahan asked.

"Homicide." Gamble seemed a little nervous. That wasn't like him. But then again, Shanahan hadn't seen him in a while. Maybe life was still a little rough. "Six months more, then I ride off into the sunset like Delaney there."

Gamble yelled at Delaney, who was down at the other end, counting gin bottles. "You should go downtown, I'm telling you, Delaney. Open up one of those go-go bars. Gotta have something to entertain the tourists."

"Keep you in business, too," Delaney said over his shoulder. His tone of voice implied more than what he actually said. "You drinkin' or what?" Delaney didn't care much for Gamble. Shanahan wasn't in love with him either, but he wasn't that bad. Sad case, more than anything. Wife with serious kidney problems and a kid that caused the policeman no end of embarrassment.

"Nah," Gamble said to the subtle suggestion to either buy a drink or leave. "Well, why not? Off duty. Among friends. A reunion of sorts. Right, Shanahan?"

"On me," Shanahan said. "Put it on the tab."

"Scotch, neat." Gamble took a deep breath. "So,

Shanahan, you didn't tell me what you're working on.
Insurance investigation? A little security work? Keeping a
diary on a randy husband?"

"I don't think I told you I was working on anything."

"That's right. You didn't. You always were tight-
lipped. Good P.I. Not like some of the other scumbuckets.
You'd a made a damned good cop, too, Shanahan."

They sat quietly for a while, listening to Delaney
count the inventory out loud.

Finally, Gamble tipped his scotch. "Well, shit Shanahan. I gotta get my car in before the mechanic goes home,
or I'm looking at an extra day in the shop." He tapped
Shanahan on the shoulder. "Listen buddy. You need some
help or something . . . anything, give me a call?"

"Right. Thanks." That wasn't like Gamble either.
However, his new cooperative attitude might be a way to
keep track of Rafferty. If he remembered right, there was
no love lost between the two cops—Gamble, a veteran
never very fast in the promotion department, and Rafferty, whose career had launched like a rocket.

"Downtown, I tell ya, Delaney!" Gamble shouted as
he went out the door.

"Another?" Delaney said to Shanahan.

"No. I have to go. I have a salad to toss."

"Is that the way you stay in shape these days?"

"Yeah. Tell Harry I said hello. I'll call him later."

"Will do."

━━━

"They were out of monkfish, so I got the orange
roughy," Maureen said. Shanahan, standing near the top
of the ladder next to the apple tree, could see her faint
outline against the screen door. "The front door was
open," she continued, "so I let myself in."

"That's why I left it open."

"That's what I thought." She came out, the wood-framed screen clacked shut behind her. It was almost sunset. The reddish light made her seem younger, prettier than he remembered. "Performing surgery?"

Shanahan's saw was halfway through a leafless limb. "Seems every spring another part of this tree goes."

"Disease?"

"Old age."

She reached up, pulled a low branch near her. "Still bears fruit," she said, fingering a tiny green apple.

"Yep."

"How do they taste?"

"I don't know." Shanahan continued to saw. "I'll be through in a minute."

"You don't eat your own apples?"

"They're pretty ugly."

"And I notice you don't grow any vegetables either. All this gardening and nothing to eat."

"That's why the good Lord made supermarkets," Shanahan said. The dead limb crashed to the ground and Casey barked at it angrily.

"Speaking of supermarkets, I bought some fresh asparagus. You like asparagus?"

"Better than frozen peas."

"What does that mean?" Maureen asked, but didn't wait for an answer. "I'll go fix the eats."

Dinner was quiet. Shanahan didn't talk much. He said he had a lot on his mind, but didn't say he was still feeling uneasy about their earlier phone conversation. She didn't press him. He liked that. Some people think they had to fill every silence with words. Shanahan called those people singers. Maureen wasn't a singer and that was a point in her favor.

At nine the phone rang. It was Harmony. He was able to get into the records. He was running the print outs now, but that would take a while, probably all night."

"Mostly bank records, it looks like, but some correspondence," Harmony said. "Also, the guy's essentially loaded a Rolodex file. Names. Addresses. Phone numbers."

"Bingo!" Shanahan said.

"I did something else," Harmony said. "No charge. I noticed that whoever this person is, he or she had a pattern. I ran a program on it. A quickie. It shows a deposit coming in of just under ten thousand dollars and the next day another transaction going out of just under ten thousand. Never quite even—odd amounts, but always just under the ten grand figure."

"Every day?"

"The fifteenth, rain or shine, a deposit. And the following day a withdrawal. I don't know what that means exactly."

"Neither do I," Shanahan said. "But it is interesting. I'll stop by tomorrow morning."

6

When the phone rang, he answered it. "Wait a minute." He laid the receiver on the nightstand so the conversation wouldn't wake Maureen. It was 2:31, according to the bright numbers on the digital clock. Maneuvering in the darkness was easy. Thirty, maybe forty years in the same house and anybody could find his way blindfolded. In the living room, he turned on the small desk lamp. It took him a moment to focus. He picked up the phone.

"Go on," Shanahan said. The hysterical voice on the other end was Mrs. Stone's.

"What more do I need to tell you, Mr. Shanahan? My house just blew up! Blew up, for God's sake!"

"When?"

"Three hours ago. Maybe more than three hours. I don't know. Knocked me to the ground. Fire spewed out and I thought it was the end of the world."

"Calm down."

"It was horrible. Who would do this? Why? Why? I can't take it. When is this going to stop?"

"Were you hurt?"

"No, I was in the backyard."

Shanahan saw the light go on in the bedroom. Maureen appeared in the doorway as he spoke. She was wrapped in the top blanket.

"Mrs. Stone, why were you in the backyard at that time of night?"

"Why are you asking me these questions, aren't you interested in *who* did it?"

"Who did it?"

"I don't know. That's why I'm paying you," she said, crying. "I have the distinct feeling that the police think I did it and I believe they think I killed Will. Now you're asking me the same questions they did. Whose side are you on?"

"Please calm down. Where are you now?"

"My sister's place."

"And where's Olivia?"

"I don't know. Wherever she stays when she isn't staying here. She said she was too upset to stay over tonight, what with Will's body found out there, and thank God she didn't."

"Were the police still there when you left?"

"They were leaving, everybody was leaving. A Lieutenant Rafferty, I think his name was, drove me to my sister's, asking sneaky questions all the way there. He wanted to know why I hired you instead of a more prestigious agency."

Shanahan wanted to know the answer to that question as well. He still didn't buy the Ouija-board theory.

"You told him."

"Yes."

"And you told him why you were out in the backyard at that time of night?"

"Yes, I told him. Wasn't I supposed to?"

"What did you tell him?" Shanahan asked, trying to be matter-of-fact about it.

"The truth."

"Yes, Mrs. Stone, I'm sure you told him the truth, but now you have to tell me the truth, because—unless you do—you'll have to rely on Rafferty to figure out the fucking thing."

Mrs. Stone started to cry again. "You don't have to use that kind of language—"

"Apparently, I do, because you are not answering my

questions. Why were you in the backyard that late at night, when most nice rich ladies are tucked in bed?"

"I couldn't sleep. . . ."

"Yes?"

"So I went out into the yard to talk to . . . to communicate with Will."

"Jesus Christ."

"Will used to go out there a lot. At night. By himself. He'd look up at the stars and some nights . . . well, he never missed a full moon. He'd be out there for a half hour, maybe an hour. His private place, you know?"

"Not all that private apparently. How do you know he did that? Did he tell you?"

"Will didn't tell me anything other than weather reports. 'Going to rain tonight,' he'd say. And I'd say 'yes, dear.' And he'd say 'time to get the oil changed in the BMW.' That's what we talked about, all we ever talked about."

"Mrs. Stone, one more time. How did you know he went out back at night?"

"I could see him from the bathroom window. On clear nights he'd walk almost down to the water and just stand there and stare. I thought that if I went out there, you know what I mean, and just waited, maybe I could talk with him and . . ." She cried.

"I understand, Mrs. Stone. I don't mean to upset you. One more question. Who else knew he did that?"

"I don't think anybody did." He could hear her sudden gasp. "Just me, I guess. Oh dear."

━━

"You want some coffee?" Maureen asked from the doorway.

"Thanks."

Maureen pulled the blanket around her as she headed for the kitchen.

"You're working on the Stone murder, aren't you?" she asked.

"How the hell did you know that?"

"Down boy! I heard about it on the car radio driving over here this evening."

"Oh?"

"Big play. They said something about a police dog uncovering the body of a missing executive in his own backyard. Ritzy address."

"Police dog?"

"Yeah, and here I thought you were retired."

"What made you think that? Because I'm old?"

"Yessir, Mr. Detective. I thought you were about six inches from the grave. That's why I'm hitting on you. Figured you leave me all your worldly possessions. My wrap, for example," she said, modeling the slightly frayed blanket. She had a way of getting to the heart of the matter.

"For the record," Maureen said, "I thought you were retired because you came to the center in the middle of the day and you didn't talk about it being your day off or where it was you worked. Most guys do, first thing. Second, I saw one of those little government window envelopes, the kind Social Security checks come in."

Shanahan was on the phone, dialing.

A hoarse voice answered.

"Harry, this is Shanahan."

"Oh, Shanahan, my pet, so nice of you to call."

"Is your van running?"

"Not at the moment, my dear Shanahan. It's all nightey-night in the garage where it is supposed to be at three o'clock in the fucking morning."

"Harry, that safe, the digital one. When the power goes off, can it be opened conventionally? I mean, can you hear the little tumblers tumble?"

"The chances are that when the power goes off, not

even the combination will open the friggin' thing. Otherwise, safecrackers would only have to shut off the power to open it. Now, if you don't mind, let's call an end to the professional consultation and I'll send you a bill in the morning. Triple time and ten percent after thirty days."

"Harry?"

"What? What?"

"What if we took the whole safe?"

"You know the story about there not bein' any such thing as military intelligence?"

"Harry?"

"What?"

"What if we got the whole safe, brought it back here and either torched it or blew the damn thing open?"

"Why don't we just take the whole house, Shanahan? Wouldn't that be easier?"

"Somebody already did, but if we're lucky, they left the safe."

———

Maureen said he looked as if he was off for the graveyard shift at a local assembly plant. All he needed, she said, was a lunch bucket and bad posture. "Good idea," Shanahan said and retrieved a battered old metal thing from the kitchen.

"By the way," she said, "I like your mustache and the new hair. You look like a Tasmanian devil."

"How many Tasmanian devils do you know?"

"Too many. But it might be fun for just one night." She had a smile full of phony seduction.

Harry's van was in the driveway. Harry, like Shanahan, wore work clothes, pretty nondescript. Harry sat at the wheel, puffing on a cigarette and wearing a Cubs cap. Shanahan handed him a name badge. Harry turned on the overhead, squinted: CITIZEN'S GAS & COKE UTILITY, WILBUR CRAPPER, SPECIAL INVESTIGATOR.

"How'd you do it?" Harry asked.

"Don't look to close. A quick cut-and-paste job. Used the stub from my gas bill and a rubber stamp."

"Let's see yours. Larry Benson. Shit, Shanahan, why'd you give me a name like Crapper?"

"Suitable name for an old fart like you."

"Like you ain't?" Harry laughed. "Haven't had so much fun since Pareee. Remember?" Harry switched off the light and the van chugged through the quiet city streets, then climbed the spiral ramp to the interstate. It would be a clean shot to the ritzy burbs at Geist.

Shanahan knew what Harry was thinking. Usually did. At the moment, Harry was thinking about France, how they pilfered a makeshift Nazi battalion headquarters. How they cracked the safe inside twenty minutes. They worked together often. Just the two of them. Most of the time, while they were in Europe, they sat in dismal hotel rooms. During that time they got to know each other real well. They could read each other's moods better than they could read their own.

They knew when to talk, when to shut up. Comfortable enough to endure each other's silences. In fact, that talent was more important than the little confessions that slipped out in the boredom or over one bottle of wine too many. Despite the war, nothing for Shanahan ever quite lived up to those days in Paris.

It was Harry who followed Shanahan back to Indiano-place, as Harry called it. Shanahan was family, the only family Harry had until he started one of his own, then another, then another.

He remembered, after the liberation, sitting at the Café Mistral with Harry. To the left were the spires of Notre Dame on that little island in the Seine. He remembered seeing the tower where Marie Antoinette was held, waiting for her head to be removed. Farther down river was the Eiffel Tower.

He remembered Jeanne, the ballet dancer. The dinner in the huge, loud restaurant called La Coupole. Her room in Les Halles. The goose bumps on her breasts in her cold room. The scratchy wool blanket on his backside and her smooth flesh beneath him. He remembered her sliding down, beneath him, her head disappearing from the pillow and her doing to him what he had only read about before. More innocent times. He had wanted to stay in Paris, wanted to live a life other than what he had chosen.

Harry talked him out of quitting the Army, staying in Paris. "Look at the retirement," he had said. "Wouldn't be the same," Harry said, "after a while the place would look like Akron." Harry reminded him of Elaine. Wasn't she pregnant and alone?

Duty. His mind raced on to Elaine, his suggesting she might do what Jeanne had done. Elaine was livid. She asked him where he learned that. Later, she asked if he'd been with other women. Shanahan evaded. She said it was all right if he had. She expected that he had while he was in Europe. He was there a long time. She was far away. He told her about Jeanne. And Elaine didn't even look at Shanahan for two weeks.

Elaine had been gone now—one way or another out of his life—for more than twenty years. But really, the memories were getting stronger, her face more vivid than it had been when they were together.

The van rolled into the driveway, behind the police car. There were no lights anywhere, but the night was clear enough for Shanahan to see that half the house still stood. Fortunately, the half that blew away was the half he wanted. It seemed the late Mr. Stone's den was the target of the blast.

"Let me do the talking, Harry."

"I wouldn't have it any other way, Sergeant Shanahan."

Shanahan was happy that Harry was enjoying himself. Across the barren platform that used to be the west end of the house, Shanahan saw a figure moving, two figures, a man and a dog.

"Not so fast fellas!" the man said.

Shanahan heard what he thought was a holster snap. And a shaft of light beamed up into his eyes.

"Glad someone's out here, gets kinda spooky, these calls in the middle of the night," Shanahan said.

"Tell your friend to get away from the truck," said the voice. The flashlight moved, catching Harry, a rolled blueprint under his arm, at the two rear doors.

"Come on around here, Wilbur. The guy probably wants to know who the hell we are. Can't say as I blame him."

"My name's Wilbur Crapper," Harry said proudly, moving in to share the light. "Gas company."

"Don't look like a gas company truck," said the officer approaching, the dog's choker chain rattling, the dog moving as the cop moved.

"Emergency call," Shanahan said. "The dispatcher said to hurry. The computer showed a hitch in the gas main in this area and they reckoned it was up here."

"Cause of the explosion earlier," Harry added.

"A hitch?" the officer asked, unbelieving.

"Well now," Shanahan said, "I could give you a scientific explanation. Just hope the damn thing don't blow while we're talking about it."

"Could take out that whole row of houses," Harry said, pointing to the other homes on the cul-de-sac, while Shanahan pulled a toothpick out of his pocket and began sucking on it.

"You have some I.D.?"

"Got my badge," Harry said.

The officer flashed his light on Harry's shirt pocket. "I'd better call in on this."

"Sure, go ahead. Mind if we back our truck outta

here, 'cause by the time you get this thing okay'd, there might not be nothin' left to call about," Harry said.

"If you want, call the dispatcher direct," Shanahan said, "might speed up the red tape."

While the policeman called, Shanahan whispered to Harry. "When we get up there and I send you back after something, put a nail in one of his rear tires."

———

Shanahan pretended to measure off the floor, while Harry unrolled the blueprints.

"Well, the cross-valve box must be here," Shanahan said. "We'd appreciate if you'd stand back a bit."

The policeman refused to move. "I like to watch."

The last thing Shanahan wanted was for the police to catch a glimpse of the dial on the safe. "'fraid it's company policy."

"This is police policy."

"Suit yourself," Harry said, pulling out a cigarette. "Got a light? On, never mind, I found it."

"What the fuck you doing, man!" Shanahan could see the cop's bug-eyed face, even in the dark.

"Hey, c'mon now, settle down. Nobody's been killed on one these things in years," Harry said, lighting up. Shanahan could see Harry's laughing eyes, and the slightest curve of a smile on his lips as the Bic let out a three-inch flame. "Except Brownie of course down there on County Line Road. Remember that? They were picking up small pieces of Brownie in both counties."

The policeman backed off a moment. Shanahan pulled back the piece of singed rug, lifted the board, then laid an old cloth over the face of the safe. "Get the small sledge, will you, Wilbur?"

Shanahan kept a running monologue with the policeman while Harry went to the truck. On his way back,

Harry lodged a small pebble in the air valve on the right rear tire of the cop car.

"What's the rag for?" the policeman asked about the cloth.

"Protect the box. Don't want dust or dirt getting in, jam up the works."

———

With each working hammer and chisel, it didn't take long to free the safe from the concrete.

"Let's see that thing," the cop said as Shanahan and Harry struggled to get it to the van. Fortunately, a call on his radio pulled him away. "I want to see that before you get out of here, you hear?"

"Sure," Shanahan said as it thunked on the metal bottom of the truck bed.

The cop, mouth to the mike, argued with someone way off in the night. Harry slid in behind the wheel of the van and Shanahan took shotgun.

"Now you wait, goddammit," the cop yelled.

"We're just getting the truck warmed up," Harry yelled out of the open window, turning on the ignition. Harry slipped it quietly into reverse, then jammed the accelerator. Screeching, the van backed into the street, stopped, then lurched forward, jerked a few times and sped off.

In the rear-view mirror, Shanahan saw the little red light go on and spin. The siren blurted out and the car limped halfway down the driveway. With the lights off, the van made the turn, and headed toward the interstate.

———

"Thanks, Maureen," Shanahan said when he came through the door. "Did anybody ever tell you what a beautiful dispatcher you are?"

"No, did anybody tell you that you're in a heap of trouble?"

"Yeah, more times than I'd like to think about. Everything went okay."

"No, it didn't."

Shanahan went into the kitchen and unscrewed the cap on the J. W. Dant bottle.

Maureen followed. "A Lieutenant Rafferty called, wanted to talk with you."

"Shit." Shanahan gulped the first shot. "What'd you say?"

"I didn't know what to say, so I said you were asleep."

"That wasn't good enough, was it?"

"No, so I had to pretend to try to wake you."

"You told him I was dead, maybe? Not good."

"I told him you were dead drunk, that I couldn't wake you up."

Shanahan reached over, pulled her to him and lifted her up in a bear hug. "You are incredible."

"You may not be very credible either," she said trying to breathe. "He's coming over to wake you up himself. All that was fifteen, twenty minutes ago."

"Shit," he dropped her to her feet.

Maureen smoothed her hair. "Thank's for the ride, but I'd rather go to Disneyland."

———

"So, who the hell are you, his wet nurse?"

Shanahan heard Rafferty's heavy-footed approach to the bedroom. The oversized cop nearly took off the door.

"Up, out of bed, you senile old bastard!"

Shanahan rolled groggily into a sitting position. He pulled the sheet toward him, squinted his eyes, pretending to focus.

"Let Rich Little do the impressions. You and some

other dickhead just made off with Stone's safe. Who was the guy with you?"

"Rafferty, oh lookee there, another nice suit. You must be making Mr. Neiman and Mr. Marcus very happy."

"I'm not in the mood for witty repartee, Shanahan. I want answers and I want them now."

Shanahan decided not to overdo the drunk bit. Do just enough to make him wonder. "Maureen, would you get me some juice, tomato juice, maybe, and an aspirin? And coffee for our guest. Or a drink maybe? But none for me. I'm sleeping."

"You won't be sleeping here, old man. The cop you conned is on his way over. And when you're fingered, I'll see to it you're deep-sixed in the Marion County jail. Now who's the other guy?"

"What other guy?"

"The guy with you tonight." Rafferty's large presence hovered over the bed.

Shanahan lifted up the sheet, pretended to look. "Well, he was here a minute ago. You must have scared him off with all that tough cop talk."

Rafferty landed an open hand on Shanahan's forehead. Light flashed and for a moment Shanahan heard nothing. Saw nothing.

"We're done with cute," Rafferty said. "An old fart like you can die in his sleep." Rafferty got up, went to the door and pushed it closed. "Now let's get serious, shall we?"

Shanahan stared straightforward. He tried to gather his thoughts. Was it all worth it? Who'd he think he was? Playing games with the police. That might have been fine twenty years ago. But he wasn't fooling anybody, except himself. This was his second case in four years. And he hadn't had a case like this in ten.

Maureen started in the door. Rafferty jerked it open so fast, it startled her.

"In the kitchen, lady, or I'll have your lovely tits in a wringer so fast . . ."

"Go on, Maureen. I'll be fine. Rafferty and I need to have a private talk. Right, Rafferty?"

Rafferty cooled. "Right. Sorry I yelled. Shanahan and I are going to work things out, aren't we Shanahan?"

"You bet."

Rafferty shut the door gently. The cop could do an about face on his emotions without blinking.

"Now you're playing smart, Shanahan. I don't like this tough-guy shit any more than you do. If you cooperate, I can make this pretty easy on you. You might not even have to serve any time. So, as I was saying, who's the other guy?"

Shanahan pulled himself to the edge of the bed and rested his head in his hands. He still felt the sting. Rafferty sat down beside him and put his hand on Shanahan's knee.

"While we're so cozy," Shanahan said slowly, "let's talk about something else first. Okay?"

"Okay"—Rafferty patted Shanahan's knee—"you start talking and I'll stop you when I don't like what you're saying. Fair enough?"

"Oh, Rafferty, you're not going to like any of this." Shanahan lifted his head, turned toward Rafferty, staring him straight in the eyes. "Let's say I have what you want."

"Don't get too comfortable with this little seating arrangement," Rafferty said, "I mean I'm a compassionate guy. . . ."

"Shove it, Rafferty. The stuff I supposedly have could come to you or it could go to other people."

"What other people?"

Shanahan wished he knew. "Mmmmn . . . other people. We'll leave it at that."

Rafferty got up, walked to the window and opened the blinds. Soft, grey light entered the room. Shanahan didn't know whether Rafferty was going to beat the shit out of him or whether the man was just thinking.

Rafferty turned. "You don't want in on this, Shanahan. Missing husbands? Yes. Murder? No. That's mine. We trade, you and I. You give me the safe and the business shit you got from Stone's computer and there won't be any charges. I can promise you that. If you don't, you will have seen about all of the golden years you're gonna see."

"I'll think about it."

"Shanahan. You were good in your day. Don't forget I know what you did during the war years. We made a file on you early on, back during the Kraft case. I mean, you were a star player. The Mickey Mantle of American Intelligence. But times change. And this isn't the old timer's All-Star game."

"I said I'll think about it."

Rafferty was at the door. "Don't think too long, pal."

Shanahan followed the lieutenant into the living room. "Good night, Shanahan." Rafferty looked tired, walked like an old man. "Good night, Miss," he said to Maureen.

Rafferty met the cop from the Stone house in the driveway and Shanahan heard Rafferty call him a dickhead.

Shanahan went toward the kitchen, poured himself two fingers of J. W. Dant.

"I didn't know you wore pajamas," Maureen kidded.

"Only when I'm entertaining." He picked up the phone, dialed, swallowed the contents of his glass. "It's Shanahan."

"Christ, somebody ought to take that phone away from you. It's a goddamn tool of torture. What do you want this time?" Harry asked, not at all happy.

"I just called to tell you not to call me."

"They make special coats for people like you."

"I figure they should have a tap in on my phone in about an hour."

"I see." Harry hung up.

——

"So what'd you tell Rafferty that made him change his tune?" Maureen asked, pulling the sheet up to her neck and snuggling up to Shanahan. The light coming in the bedroom window was pink.

"I don't know exactly."

"Have you ever made love by the dawn's early light?" Maureen asked.

"Sounds pretty patriotic."

"You feeling a little patriotism at the moment?"

"A man's got to believe in something."

7

Afterward, he couldn't sleep. He left Maureen in bed, her body curved beneath the soft folds of the sheet. The light through the blinds made zebra stripes on the white cotton.

Quietly, he went to the kitchen, opened the door to the landing and went downstairs. It was cool, damp. He turned on the light. Seven or eight water bugs scampered off to the corners. He went over to what used to be the coal room before they converted the heat to gas, pulled the string and the naked bulb lit the room, dangled a few seconds, whirling shadows in the windowless space. Shanahan found the right shelf and pulled down a box.

He used his hand to wipe off the dust. He undid the string tied around the box and lifted the lid. Both the box and the contents were slightly damp and smelled of mildew. Shanahan squatted on the floor, his back against the concrete block wall. He felt like a kid in his secret playroom. He hadn't been down there in years.

He pulled out the black album. It was falling apart. He looked at the old photographs, more brown and white than black-and-white. Little photos. He remembered some of them were taken with one of those miniature German cameras. Elaine in her parents' backyard, sitting in a white Adirondack chair, smiling, slightly embarrassed, holding a glass of lemonade. Behind her, the peonies were in bloom. He remembered getting a start on his own peonies from their garden.

She looked like she did in his dream, the one in which she waved good-bye to him. How young she was. How slender. God, they had waited until the honeymoon, hadn't they? That was the first time he saw and touched her small, firm breasts. How easy it was, the two of them, making love. Two glasses of wine and she couldn't wait to get back to the hotel room. San Diego. The first time, her body was ivory. By the time the trip was done, he could feel the sun's heat come from her tanned body as he pressed down on her.

"Let's do it every night and every morning," she said. "I didn't know it was going to be this good."

Different times. He was virgin, too, despite every attempt by his buddies to get him into a Terre Haute whorehouse. He was glad then. No one, he thought, was as beautiful as Elaine. Not Betty Grable. Not Rita Hayworth. And certainly not the girls on Cherry Street in Terre Haute.

Meeting Elaine was all accident. He met her mother first. A pretty woman. Shanahan had stopped at a little Lutheran Church in downtown Indianapolis. Home on leave, he had wandered down to a movie and had an hour to kill. To get out of the heat, he went into the church.

In uniform, he attracted quite a bit of attention. Elaine's mom introduced herself. They talked. She invited him back to the house, to join the family for their ritual Sunday dinner. He couldn't think quick enough to refuse. Funny, he hadn't thought about Elaine's mother in years. She had a sense of humor. So did Elaine early on. The father was serious, maybe even slightly pompous. He meant well. Over dinner, Shanahan remembered Dad Sawyer launching into his economic theory of war. Elaine rescued him, took him out into the backyard. They talked. He'd never met a woman he could talk with before Elaine. Somehow, then at least, she could draw him out.

Shanahan flipped through the pages. He shouldn't have. He could see everything falling apart. He could see it in the photographs as they got more recent. They told a story, didn't they? There were smiles now and again on the faces in those photographs. They just got phonier and phonier.

————

Outside, in the back garden, Shanahan picked the young clover and dandelions sprouting from the lily bed while the soil was still moist from the dew. Life seemed gentle and precious this morning. Change or die. He had allowed change, hadn't he? There was Maureen. There was the man he'd never met, whose existence meant nothing to him, whose death now threatened him.

No backing out now. Unless Shanahan put all the pieces together first, Rafferty would have his ass one way or another—rotting away in a prison cell or dead. Shanahan needed to get with Harmony to look over Stone's business records and he needed to get with Harry to find out what was in the safe. But Rafferty would have someone watching, someone or two someones or maybe several someones, depending on just how important this murder really was. Already, Shanahan wasn't a free man. He didn't dare use his phone. And he'd be followed.

The quiet was broken by twigs snapping in the hedge behind him. Shanahan turned, saw Casey streaking after a squirrel and about to overtake him. Suddenly another squirrel streaked across Casey's path and in a moment of confusion, Casey lost them both. One of the squirrels, now safely out of reach in the bow of a tree, was leaning down and giving Shanahan's dog a good bawling out.

————

He couldn't leave until the stores opened downtown. He sat in one of the two Adirondack chairs in the backyard. Maureen was in the other with a cup of coffee. The peonies were little white buds. They'd be in full bloom on Memorial Day. It had been that way forever.

Race day and peonies. The small redbud was no longer pink and not a very inspiring tree after April.

"I like it here," Maureen said.

"I like you being here."

"Do you? I hope you do." Maureen spoke softly, hesitantly. "It's only fair to tell you I'm making plans."

"For what?"

"To move in with you." She caught herself. "I mean I'm thinking about it."

Shanahan was quiet. He'd thought about it. But he had no idea the subject would come up so fast.

"I warned you I'm a pushy broad. Am I scaring the hell out of you?"

"Yeah," Shanahan said. "You are."

"How far out of line am I? Asking you now."

"I don't know. A week, two weeks maybe." Years went by. Nothing happened. In the last few days, everything's happened. Elaine dies. He snubs a son he hasn't seen in twenty-five years. The guy he looks for is dead and a house is blown to smithereens. Then Rafferty comes along and threatens to put him in a cage for the rest of his natural life. Now, this forty-three-year-old, very attractive woman wants to move in.

"There's no point in long engagements at my age," Shanahan said. "But I'd appreciate it if we didn't make any real commitments until some of this other stuff gets settled."

"That's fair." Maureen picked up the dirty tennis ball lying at her feet, tossed it. Casey took off, leaping. Caught it on the first bounce and brought it back to her. "I just thought I ought to let you know what was going on in my mind. Give you a chance to dodge the arrow."

She tossed the ball again. Casey leapt gracefully, catching it in mid-flight. "He could play third base," she said.

"No." Shanahan shrugged. "He can't throw worth a damn."

———

There were four of them, all roughly the same size, standing around Shanahan's bathroom at 10:15 a.m. the next morning. They had been ordered to march through the shower. They had shaved and now Maureen was doing a little hair trimming, while Shanahan took the price tags and pins out of their four matching sets of shirts and trousers.

Shanahan had picked the guys up at University Park, in clear view of the guys inside the unmarked cop car who followed Shanahan's Malibu down and back.

Two of his new recruits were out of work and killing time in the park. The other two weren't looking for work; sobered from the night before, they were glad to get the twenty bucks so they could go on a roar that night.

"I don't get it," said the guy trying on the pair of grey work pants. "Who's the joke supposed to be on?"

"You're the one who has the driver's license?" Shanahan asked, ignoring the question.

"Yessir, for forty years and never one accident. 'Course I never had a car."

"Are you sure you can drive?"

"I'm just funnin' ya. Drove all my life. Milk trucks, bread trucks, dry cleaners and newspaper trucks. Still drive a cab once in a while."

"You know what you're supposed to do?"

"It's pretty crazy, but I remember. I drive downtown to the parking garage on Maryland Street, take a ticket, park the car and then all us guys split, go in different directions."

"The keys to the car?"

"I know, I know. I drop 'em underneath the seat and lock the car."

"Right. And when you pull into the parking garage?"

"I stop the car, you get out real quick, and I drive on up to the top floor."

"Here," said Shanahan, passing out identical straw hats, "don't forget these."

———

They worked out the Keystone Cop routine because Shanahan wasn't so sure there wasn't a stooge with a pair of binoculars on a rooftop somewhere in the neighborhood. At first, the four guys thought Shanahan was crazy. Then, they started enjoying it. Doing the Groucho walk.

All four of the identically dressed comedians went out to the car. Shanahan got in back, crawled behind the driver's seat and, hidden from prying eyes, removed his dress-alike clothes. Two got out of the car and went into the house. One came out, then another, then two went from the car to the house. The routine went on for about ten minutes until any observer would go crazy trying to figure it all out. When the car backed out of the drive, four people could be seen heading down Washington Street heading downtown.

"Hey, we got ourselves a tail," the driver said. "Zat what you wanted?"

"Absolutely," Shanahan said, smiling. "You're pretty quick in these matters, eh?"

"Well, sometimes the cars I'd drive, you know, they wasn't zactly mine."

When the car pulled into the parking garage, Shanahan, who during various painful contortions had managed to remove the look-alike clothes, was now dressed in a dark suit, white shirt and red tie.

Shanahan would have liked to have seen their faces—Rafferty's men, trying like hell to follow four Shanahans and not knowing he wasn't any of them. In the parking garage, he waited a few minutes in the restroom, straightening his tie. He patted his cheeks with some cold water. He could have been a bank president. No, his face was a little too weathered for the soft life.

He crossed the street to the Hyatt, found the telephones in the lobby and called Harry. Not home. It was eleven-thirty. If the Cubs had an early game, Harry could be at Delaney's bar, watching the pre-game show. He'd catch Harry there later. He called his own number. Maureen answered. "How about dinner?" he asked her.

"Your turn to cook," she said.

"The King Cole?"

"Suddenly you're a millionaire?"

"No. But I've got a VISA and my eighty-five dollars a day is mounting up. Meet you there at eight."

"Oooh la-la." Maureen said. "You gotta date, Daddy Warbucks."

Shanahan called Harmony and told him he'd be over in half an hour if that was all right. It was. Shanahan rented a car in the hotel, a cream-colored Lincoln Towne Car, stopped at Ayres to buy a briefcase and drove to Fountain Square to pick up the computer print outs. They were a gold mine. He had the address of Stone's attorney, accountant, several banks and businesses, plus one Mr. Samuel Kessler. There were also detailed bank statements.

"Good stuff?" Harmony asked, seeing the smile on Shanahan's face.

"Real good. I really appreciate what you've done." Shanahan said, dropping the computer reports and discs in his new briefcase. "What do I owe you?"

"Nothing. This was for Harry, but you have to promise to let me know how all of this comes out. Your case and all."

"This is business, Harmony. I demand a bill. It will be charged to the client and she is quite able to pay. But do me a favor and don't send it to my house until I call you.

I don't want anybody tracing this back to you. May I use your phone?"

Shanahan dialed Delaney's, found Harry. "What was in the safe?"

"You won't believe this, but hardly anything," Harry said. "Three videotapes and a stack of letters. No cash, no policies, no nothin'."

"I should be by about five. Can you have the stuff there?"

"Where?"

"Where you are right now."

"Shanahan, if I wait that long I'll be shit-faced."

"Leave 'em with Delaney. Tell him to give them to no one but me."

"The game's gonna start any minute."

"Stop whining, Harry. You're on the payroll. And if we don't find out what's going on, you could get on the bad side of a nasty cop."

———

The lawyer's office was near Lockerbie. Shanahan hadn't been in that neighborhood since they turned the squalid turn-of-the-century homes into something quaint and expensive. The Lincoln took the cobblestones in stride. The firm was in an old Victorian, the brick had been re-pointed, the shutters refurbished.

Inside, a woman watered an ancient fern. "I'm here to see the attorney handling the affairs of William B. Stone. Would that be a Mr. Bindley or Mr. Bosworth or Mr. Moore?" he said, repeating the names he saw on the brass plaque next to the door.

"That could be Mr. Bindley, Mr. Bosworth or Mrs. Moore."

"Sorry, I usually keep my chauvinism under wraps."

She was an attractive woman, dark with brown eyes and extremely short pitch-black hair. Her dress was black and she wore huge pieces of jewelry. American Indian, it appeared.

"I'm the Moore and I handle Mr. Stone's legal affairs." She smiled, almost flirting. "And just who might you be?"

"I'm Mrs. Stone's brother-in-law," Shanahan said. He had been taken back enough to have nearly blown his line.

"I've never met *Mrs*. Stone," the woman said. "How is she taking it?"

"Shocked, confused, homeless."

"I understand. What can I do for you?"

"Among other things," Shanahan said, "Mrs. Stone has no idea how she's being taken care of . . . financially. Mr. Stone, I'm afraid, left her pretty much in the dark."

"And?" she asked, still holding the watering can.

"And, I wondered if you could give me a little bit of information about wills, insurance, anything that might give her a clue about her future."

"I don't know, Mr. . . ."

"Shanahan. Dietrich Shanahan."

"Will was a pretty private person and legally, I'm not sure that I can divulge this at the moment. I need to think about it and probably should discuss this with Mrs. Stone directly. No offense."

"The problem is, Mrs. Moore, she doesn't understand financial matters very well. She asked me to stop by, begged me to. On top of everything else, she's not sure if she's heading to the poorhouse. She doesn't need a complete rundown. Just an idea."

"Well, all right. Follow me," she said and headed into a room beyond the entry hall. Her office wasn't all that big, probably used to be a parlor. There was a small fireplace. A white, overstuffed sofa took up most of the room. There was a matching white chair, a small desk. Through a second door, Shanahan could see another room where piles of paper lay on top of a large mahogany table. A man sat at one end of the table, shirt-sleeves rolled up, tie loosened going over a stack.

"You'll have to pardon me, Mr. Shanahan, but I don't understand how women today, especially educated ones, can go through life without knowing something about their own affairs. It's ridiculous." Shanahan didn't say anything. "Don't get me wrong. I feel very sorry for them and especially Mrs. Stone, losing her husband, then her house. That's the only reason I'm doing this. So what I tell you is strictly off the record."

Shanahan sat down in the white chair. He was amused by the more elegant world he pretended to live in. Just be Tyrone Power, he told himself.

"I understand, Mrs. Moore. I sincerely appreciate any light you could possibly shed on Mrs. Stone's financial future." He wasn't sure where this educated tone and these formal words came from. He wasn't doing too bad.

"The irony is," the woman said, putting on a pair of oversized blue-rimmed glasses, sighing deeply, "Will was changing everything. His will, his insurance . . . that is to say the primary beneficiary was being changed."

"You mean that Mrs. Stone isn't the beneficiary?"

"Actually she is, but if Mr. Stone had been able to keep his appointment Monday, she wouldn't have gotten all that much. Enough to take care of her, comfortably, but the bulk of the estate was to go to someone else."

"To whom?" Shanahan asked, remembering not to say "to who."

She paused a moment, then suddenly said, "Todd Marquette. Do you have any idea who he is?"

"No, I'm afraid not."

"I'm afraid I don't either. That's why I asked," she said, standing up. "As it stands then, unless the will is contested by this Mr. Marquette, she will receive somewhere in the neighborhood of a million in life insurance, plus dividends and the tangible assets of the estate. Mr.

Stone was worth a considerable amount of money. All of this plus whatever she has in her own name."

"Oh, I don't think that amounts to much," Shanahan said.

"Really?" the attorney asked, surprised or doubtful. Shanahan wasn't sure which. "At any rate, if she hires a competent accountant, she'll have no worries. It would be hard to spend it all."

8

Could Mrs. Stone have known about the changes her husband intended to make? Was she capable of killing her husband or perhaps hiring someone else to do it? After making a stop at Central Library to check out the Marquettes in the phone book and finding none, Shanahan cruised north, up Meridian Street on his way to meet Kessler.

These people lived in another world. He thought of Mrs. Moore's office. Mrs. Stone's home. The environment they created for themselves. Shanahan felt like an interloper. Then again, he was, wasn't he? And he was enjoying himself.

If Geist and Carmel were prestigious areas, this part of Meridian Street represented older money. Expansive stone or brick mansions, built in the twenties and thirties. Long, perfectly landscaped lawns, large enough for regulation football, separated the homes from the tree-lined street. This was where the governor lived, where the decorator show houses were. Behind these houses were swimming pools, tennis courts, and four-car garages with servants quarters above them. Hell, they had bathrooms the size of his entire house.

He had a few more miles to go. To 116th street, where the Indiana farmlands were transformed into marble-faced office buildings surrounded by golf-course lawns, dotted by fountains. What family farms didn't get swallowed up by megabucks corporate farmers were gobbled up by huge campus headquarters of major corporations. This was the BMW brigade, where the word *country* had nothing to do with cornfields or Dolly Parton.

Shanahan didn't believe Mrs. Stone would have, could have done it. If she had, why did she hire him? He didn't like one of the plausible answers.

———

This was turning out to be a busy day. Shanahan walked through a packed parking lot to the contemporary brick office complex. Closer to the building were the private parking places. No Ford Escorts here. Just Mercedes, BMW's and Audi 5000's. These were the cars of the super preppies—the coffee achievers. Not landed gentry, but the landing gentry, who did everything in the name of investment or appreciation or tax incentive.

"Do you have an appointment with Mr. Kessler?" the young woman asked, pulling politeness out of a can.

"No, but I'm sure he would find it beneficial to talk with me. I'll only be a couple of minutes."

"Your card?"

"Please just tell him . . ."

"May I tell him whom you represent." She showed no impatience. Her job was to screen people. Just a crisp business attitude. She wasn't about to piss off somebody important, but she wasn't about to waste her boss's valuable time with typewriter-ribbon salesmen. She looked pro. A handsome jacket and one of those bow ties women wear when they prefer aspiration to perspiration.

"Tell Mr. Kessler I represent William B. Stone," Shanahan said, watching her eyes to see if she recognized the name. Not a blink.

"Please take a seat and I'll be right back with you." She disappeared behind a door, closing it softly behind her.

Shanahan sat down. Across the room was a large painting. Broad swirls of color in gray and mauve to blend with the walls and plush carpeting. To his right on the table were magazines. *Forbes, Fortune, Business Week.* At the bottom of the pile of magazines, there were some newsletters on expensive paper from, or about, the Securities and Exchange Commission. There was a pamphlet that talked about U.S. investment opportunities in Central and South America.

He picked up the morning paper. It had headlines on the Circle Centre project, a story on the drug war, and the fact that Indianapolis was being considered as a future Olympics site. There were the Indianapolis 500 qualifiers, a joke, capsule weather and a biblical quote or two, but nothing on Stone's death or his house blowing up. The city was too busy celebrating its emergence on the national scene to feature a murder of one of its civic lights. But you'd think the conservative paper would canonize a fellow Republican, followed by a call-to-action editorial to solve this most heinous crime. Curious.

When Miss Junior Exec ushered Shanahan into the office, Kessler didn't get up. He was on the phone. He motioned for Shanahan to sit down, then swiveled his chair 180 degrees. The window he now faced overlooked the parking lot. Kessler kept his voice low. Occasionally Shanahan could make out a phrase: "Where are they going to get that kind of money?" or "Not by the time they adjust the income."

Shanahan let his eyes roam. The office looked cheap, but it wasn't. A corner office, loads of blond furniture trimmed in brass. A Leroy Neiman original of a golfer in mid-swing. Looked like the rental office for an expensive condominium complex in La Jolla. White on white everywhere.

Kessler, at first glance in his dark suit, white shirt and red tie, looked a little too Eastern uptight for his California laid-back office. Shanahan looked at his own black suit, white shirt and red tie. Twins. The power look.

The executive's voice raised angrily. "If I could be everywhere then I wouldn't have to pay you, would I? If

I come down . . ." Kessler's voice trailed back into a whisper.

The photographs on Kessler's desk were family, the frames turned in such a way that visitors would have to look at Kessler's wife and offspring more than he did. There was a faded color photograph of Kessler and a woman Shanahan presumed to be the wife. Kessler smiling, looking directly into the camera. Probably taken shortly before or after the marriage. Kessler had put on quite a few pounds since. He looked bloated now. There was another photograph of Kessler, the same woman and two boys. It showed Kessler a little heavier, but not like he was now. The smiles on the second picture seemed a little forced. It reminded Shanahan of his own photographs. Snapshots can tell stories.

Kessler swiveled halfway round. "At the rate we're going, we're not going to make enough on this deal to pay for the phone call and I've got somebody sitting here. So see what you can salvage, amigo." Kessler's "amigo" wasn't exactly friendly.

"Look," Kessler said, not bothering even a glance at Shanahan, "I don't know what this is all about, but I haven't seen Stone in years."

"Mr. Kessler, I'm trying to learn what I can about Stone's past and I believe you can fill a couple of holes."

Kessler swiveled now to face his desk, but his eyes never met Shanahan's. "So, who are you?"

"I'm a private investigator, working for Mrs. Stone."

The corpulent exec with the avoiding eyes leaned way back in his chair, looked up to the ceiling in a kind of God-deliver-me gesture. "I've got nothing to talk to you about and I've got too much to do to take time for a little sentimental chit chat."

"Mrs. Stone is very distressed," Shanahan said, hoping that even a little phony concern on Kessler's part might reveal something.

"Mrs. Stone is a crackpot. She's always distressed."

"Just a couple of questions. I'll be out of here before you know it."

"I don't think you catch on too quick."

"Could be. However, I did catch something going through Stone's papers that leads me to believe you and he had a special interest in Central America." Shanahan was fishing. It was the only thing he knew about the man.

Kessler's eyes flashed directly at Shanahan and for a split second, there was eyeball to eyeball contact.

"Stone and I dissolved our partnership a long, long time ago. It's all history. So's our little meeting, Mr."—he looked down at the note on the desk—"Shanahan." Kessler swiveled his chair so he was again facing the window.

"Helluva a nice guy," Shanahan said to the secretary as he left.

She didn't flinch. She had the kind of attitude that people have sometimes when they work for somebody they think powerful. They believe they are an extension of the power. She showed a perfect poker face and spoke to him as if she were telling him how to get home after his first day in kindergarten. "Good-bye, Mr. Shanahan, have a nice afternoon." She had to appear to be nice.

Shanahan didn't. "I think Sam's plants need watering. Be a good girl, will ya?"

Still another stop. This time at Delaney's bar. Delaney's place didn't have an official name, nothing over the top of the door. You knew it was a bar because of the neon beer signs in the window. Inside, Harry would be waiting. If the Cubs were playing at Wrigley Field—and Shanahan had lost track of where they'd be for the first time in three years—it would probably be a day game. Despite the new lights, there were few night games at

Wrigley. Shanahan hated the idea of Wrigley all lit up. Baseball was supposed to be played in the afternoons and definitely outside under blue skies and on real, green grass. Harry would be sitting in a dark, cool bar sipping on a Stroh's, watching to see how today's boys of summer compared with Ted Williams and Musial and Ernie Banks.

"It's never easy," Harry said, dipping his onion rings in the catsup. "Extra goddamned innings. Christ be Jesus, they're enough to give you a heart attack." Sometimes Harry hated the Cubs, but he'd never give up on them.

The other Harry, Harry Caray, the long time Cubs announcer, was talking about the MacMurray family from South Bend, Indiana, coming over to see the game. The great Harry Caray who returned to his post after a heart attack. The President of the United States called and wished him well. The mayor proclaimed it Harry Caray Day in Chicago. Harry Caray, a genuine old-timer. Something to be said for old-timers. Then again, Reagan was an old-timer, wasn't he? Shot that theory. The guy couldn't manage left field.

Shanahan slid in on the other side of the booth, stole an onion ring. Delaney had Shanahan's beer in front of him before his rear end hit the cushion.

"Damn, Shanahan, you been to a funeral?" Delaney asked.

"Deets here is mixin' with the rich and famous nowadays, Delaney," Harry said. "Sittin' over there and can't even see the game. Move over here, Deets. This is a nail biter."

"D'jeet?" Delaney asked, wiping his hands on his apron. "Got some stew left. Enough for one. Don't want it to spoil, so it's on the house."

"Thanks, Delaney, but I'm going out later."

"Where you going?" Harry asked as the bartender went back to the bar, cocked one foot up and stared at the TV screen.

"Having dinner with someone."

"Where you going?" Harry repeated.

"Out."

"You're getting awful mysterious these days, Deets. Going over to Hagerstown for some catfish?"

"No. What did you find in the safe?"

"I'm not telling, till you tell."

"You're acting like a kid, Harry."

"I am a kid. Never grew up. Don't have any plans to. So, tell me and I'll tell you.

"The King Cole with a friend."

"The King Cole. Now ain't that something? With a friend," Harry said, nodding his head. "Now isn't that sweet? Delaney!" Harry yelled, "Deets here is goin' to the King Cole tonight with a friend. Don't that beat all."

"Oooh-whee!" Delaney said, "no wonder he passed on a bit of Delaney's regular, old, everyday beef stew."

"Harry, what did you find in the safe?"

"Who you goin' with, Lady Di?"

"Harry, if you don't tell me what I want to know, I'm going to cut your balls off and put them in Delaney's stew."

"I found"—Harry reached beside him and pulled out some papers—"a stack of letters. Didn't read 'em. Well, I read one. It was a little mushy and I was feeling pretty sleazy reading it, so I stopped. And I found two video-tapes. Didn't watch 'em."

"That's all?"

"That's all. No money, no jewelry, no important papers. Most boring safe job I ever done." He shoved the stuff across the table to Shanahan, who stuffed them in his already stuffed briefcase. "So what do you think is going on with the Stone thing?"

"So far, just a nasty businessman named Kessler who won't talk but is pretty touchy about Central America."

Harry shook his head.

"And the fact that Stone was in the middle of changing his will and the beneficiary on his life insurance policy to some guy named Marquette."

"Who's he?"

"Have no idea. Not in the book, not in any of Stone's computer files. The mystery man."

"So Stone was freezin' out the little lady."

"Yep."

"She know that?"

"I don't think so, but I don't know."

"But that puts the heat on her fanny, don't it?"

"Yeah."

"Your very own client," Harry said, not looking at the game. "How much sense does that make? Why would she hire a detective to find out who did it . . . if she did it?"

"Could be a diversion. Find some old, incompetent detective and tell the jury that if she had murdered her husband, she wouldn't have hired a detective to find out who did?"

"You're not old. Hell, you're younger than I am," Harry said angrily.

"That doesn't make me Shirley Temple."

"Shirley Temple is older than I am," Harry said.

———

Maureen was beautiful. Sitting at the table, sipping her wine, auburn hair loose around her neck, a slender jape droplet on a fine gold chain. Shanahan wanted to tell her how beautiful she was. Saying things like that wasn't easy for him. Maybe he should do it kiddingly: "You sure clean up nice." No, that was all wrong.

"Aren't you going to tell me how beautiful I am?" Maureen asked, smiling.

"No, I'm not going to tell you," Shanahan said, "but you are, you know."

"You're beautiful, too. Handsome I mean."

"What? Is that something less than beautiful?"

Maureen smiled at him. He looked around the restaurant. The place wasn't as overdone as he thought it would be. Just stodgy. Old oil paintings, portraits mostly, of stodgy men wearing wigs and prune-faced women in black. Sixteen hundred they were painted, maybe. What did he know of such things? The wood-paneled walls reminded him of Stone's study.

He took a bite of his salad. Somebody had screwed up the vinegar and oil with mayonnaise. "Normally, I'd feel a little out of place here." Shanahan would rather have gone to St. Elmo's. It wouldn't have been much cheaper, just less pretentious. "I don't feel out of place, though. I think it's because you're here."

The waiter removed the salad plates, then replenished the wine glasses.

"Not to show ingratitude, because I am enjoying myself . . . very much . . ."

"Yes?" Shanahan encouraged her. "You want to know why we're here. Right?"

"Yes."

"I'm dressed up in my one nice suit. I rented a Lincoln Towne Car. I'm working, making a little money and . . ."

"And?"

"And when Rafferty shows up, I'll know my phone's tapped and I don't want him flouncing his thousand-buck European suit at me while I'm munching a burger at Bill's Diner."

"He hit you, didn't he . . . in the bedroom?"

"I haven't forgotten. It had me down for a few minutes, had me talking to myself as a matter of fact. It made me feel like I should go ahead and crawl into my grave."

"You don't feel that way now."

"No, I don't."

The main course arrived. He tried to avoid thinking

how expensive it was. It's natural on a fixed income, but goddammit this was a special night, a celebration of sorts and he was here with a beautiful woman.

"Your phone is tapped, Shanahan," Maureen said, looking over her dinner companion's shoulder. "He's here, talking to the maître d'."

Shanahan didn't look as Rafferty kibitzed with the headwaiter, then wound his way through the tables, stopping twice, making lengthy conversation with people at other tables.

"He's quite a gadabout," Maureen said, "knows a lot of people. Not bad company for a cop."

"He has aspirations," Shanahan said. "Chief of Police, probably. With the people involved in this case, Rafferty could suddenly shoot up the ladder, or, if he screws up, embarrasses the wrong people, he could be blown right off the rungs."

Shanahan had the second sliver of sole to go, when Rafferty edged over to the table.

"Hope I'm not intruding," he said, then not giving Shanahan a chance to say he was, "but I thought I ought to warn you."

"The British are coming?"

"No, your case, Shanahan." He glanced at Maureen. "You look lovely."

Maureen glared. "You look prosperous."

"Or preposterous, but that's beside the point. I'm not here to win friends and influence people," Rafferty said.

"Could have fooled me," Maureen said.

"It was nice of you to drop by, Rafferty, but I'm sure you've got places to go and people to see."

"I just thought you ought to know that if you plan to have Mrs. Stone pay for your night on the town, you could be in way over your head. We're booking her for murder."

"Whose?" Shanahan asked. "She run over a rampaging socialite?"

"Shanahan, it's pretty clear she iced hubby," Rafferty said. His face suggested he'd just swallowed something larger than a canary.

"Do you believe that or is it simply easier to pin it on her and get this embarrassing situation cleared up?"

"We've got it all, Shanahan. Motive! Talked with one Mrs. Moore. You know her, don't you? The pretty lawyer? She called us after she talked to you. Seems as if Mrs. Stone was about to be disinherited. Corpse! Stone himself dead, buried in his own backyard. Weapon. Stone's thirty-two found in the rubble. That's enough, but we're working on a witness, could be an eyewitness."

"Who's that?"

"Confidential. Incidentally, my boys got a kick out of your magic tricks this afternoon."

"I'll bet they did. I don't like tails, Rafferty. Or wiretaps."

"I'm afraid that's the luck of the Irish, Shanahan. And if I were you, I wouldn't play hardball with the boys. They get pretty excited. Get carried away. You might find it pretty hard to get through the day without a traffic ticket. Maybe a citation for reckless driving, drunken driving. I know you catch my drift."

"Certainly. I can't wait for the tide to go out." Shanahan shoved his plate toward Rafferty and said drily, "You want the rest of this?"

"No thanks."

"Keep up your strength. Excuse me!" Shanahan said to the waiter, "would you get the nice policeman a doggy bag."

"Cut the comedy, Shanahan."

The waiter looked puzzled. "Go ahead," Shanahan said.

"I'll take the plate back to the kitchen, sir."

"No, just the doggy bag, a big one."

"Yessir."

"I'd be very careful," Shanahan said to Rafferty. "Mrs. Stone didn't do it. I think you know that."

"I don't know any such thing," Rafferty said, grinning. "But I do know I can pull your chain whenever I want. There is the matter of the safe."

"Who said there was anything in it?" Shanahan said. "You found the insurance policies and Stone's very last will and testament."

"You're telling me the safe was empty?" Rafferty wasn't buying it.

"Am I? I don't recall telling you I had the safe."

"I got a cop who can I.D. you."

"You do?" Shanahan wasn't buying it.

"To be honest—"

"For a change—"

"You don't fit the description, but then you have a thing for masquerades. Costumes."

When the waiter returned, Shanahan took the bag and filled it with the little computer discs from his briefcase. "There's something in there that might change your mind about hanging this on her."

"And what might that be?" Rafferty asked, looking Shanahan square in the eyes.

"Confidential."

"You withholding evidence?"

"No." Shanahan handed him the white paper sack. "Here it is. Now you're holding the bag."

It was such a strain to smile, Rafferty could have gotten a charley horse in his cheek muscles. But he smiled and left.

"What's in there that's going to change his mind about Mrs. Stone?" Maureen asked.

"I wish I knew."

"You'd be hell in a poker game. I thought you were serious."

"I was, in a way. There's a funny thing about one of his bank accounts. Every month there's a deposit of nine thousand something dollars and the next day there's money going out in a similar but not exact amount. According to the codes, they're cash transactions. Seems strange that he'd be dealing with cash."

"The amounts were close to but never more than ten thousand dollars?"

Shanahan nodded. "I don't know what it means, but it's interesting."

"It probably means that he was trying to hide the transactions from the IRS. Banks have to report cash transactions of ten thousand dollars and over."

"How do you know that?"

"I used to work for a bank, auditor, about to be a senior auditor when . . ."

It was obvious she was headed in a direction she didn't want to go. He thought he ought to change the subject. "What else did you used to do?"

"Lots of things. I taught. High school math. I waited tables, washed dishes, took my clothes off at the Red Garter. And now, I'm . . . a physical therapist."

"You mean to say a guy deposits more than ten thousand dollars in cash one day and he gets reported, but he can deposit nine-thousand nine-hundred and ninety-nine dollars every business day of the year and not get reported?"

"Not exactly, but it's harder to catch."

9

Shanahan felt good. Even though he felt no closer to figuring out who killed Stone and why, he knew he had picked up a lot of the pieces today. Maybe taking pleasure in making fools of Rafferty's boys wasn't the most mature of emotions, but it was more fun than baseball. So was playing with Rafferty at dinner. He wasn't done with Rafferty. Normally, Shanahan didn't hold a grudge, but this was an exception. Rafferty would pay.

"I'm working on becoming a habit," Maureen said, snuggling against Shanahan. She lowered the sheet that covered them and ran her fingers over his chest. "If you want me to spend a night or two away from here, you'll have to tell me."

Shanahan was thinking. Ideas seemed to come better to him in the dark, in the quiet.

"Let's just lie here, quiet for awhile." He expected her to roll away from him and sulk. That's what Elaine would have done, letting out one of those painful sighs. Maureen didn't. But then again, she didn't shut up.

"Just one more thing before I become a pillar of salt," Maureen said. "I really feel sorry for the other woman."

"What other woman?"

"Stone's. She really loved him. Moved to be near him. There wasn't one nagging letter about Stone leaving his wife, did you notice that?"

Shanahan and Maureen had sat at the kitchen table before going to bed, reading the letters found in Stone's safe. They would have played the tapes, but Shanahan's VCR was VHS. The cassettes were Beta.

The letters were signed "WAML." It was Maureen

who thought it probably meant "with all my love." No names anywhere. Discreet. The return addresses were torn from the envelopes. The postmarks weren't. The earlier letters, dating back eight years, were sent from San Francisco. They were the most frequent, roughly one a week. They were also the most optimistic, the most supportive. "You are what you are," the writer had said, "and there's nothing wrong with that. I can understand you're not wanting to leave your wife. If that means I must move there to be with you and enjoy whatever time you can manage, I will. I wait only for your invitation. An evening, even a moment, now and then, can sustain me."

The last five years worth of letters had an Indianapolis postmark. There were only a few of those. On all of them, the salutation was simply "My Dear L," which could have been a first initial if the letters weren't intended for Will Stone. But the likelihood was that the "L" stood for love or lover.

The last letter was the most interesting:

Dear L,

We're funny people, you and I. Loners. Like you, I've always been alone, but until now, never lonely. Never being able to look forward to an evening together is like losing all my senses at once. And I've lived here so long, I cannot even go home. Home is gone now. Or it is here.

I'm not trying to make you feel guilty. But you must understand. If I didn't tell you how much I love you, that you are still my life, as you have been since we met, I would forever wonder if I had done everything possible to keep this alive. I would forever wonder if your decision was based on some foolish misunderstanding. I've never liked the tragedy of Romeo and Juliet.

It is true that I have slept with other people. I didn't, you know, for a long time. Sometimes, a person needs the warmth of another body. That is all it was. My heart, my soul, my spirit, all were with you always. They still are.

Please talk to me. You owe nothing. Not even conversation.

Perhaps, after so many, I am asking you for one last gift. A moment of your time.

WAML

"I think he probably loved her too," Shanahan said finally.

"Did you ever cheat on your wife?" Maureen asked.

"Once. How'd you know I was married?"

"This was her house—I mean, where the two of you lived. You'd have never bought this bedspread or those draperies."

"I could have lived with my mother."

"Not you."

"Did you ever cheat on your husband?" Shanahan asked, not caring but wondering how honest she'd be.

"So, Mr. Detective, how did you know I was married?"

"Figured it. That's all. At least once."

"A wild guess. You call it a hunch, huh?"

"What were the circumstances?" Shanahan asked.

"What circumstances?"

"When you cheated."

"Met a nice older man. Gave him a massage, invited myself over to his place."

"Sounds familiar."

"It should." Maureen ran her fingers over Shanahan's brow, traced the outline of his nose.

"Me?"

"Who else?"

"You're still married?" Shanahan rolled over, looked down at her. He could barely make out her smile in the darkness.

"I don't know where he is, though. Walked out."

Shanahan thought of Stone. Wondered if Maureen's husband had a mouthful of earth. "Do you think he's alive?"

"He's preaching somewhere . . . on the move, the big black book and plenty of hell fire and brimstone."

"You married a preacher?" It didn't seem likely.

"I married a cigarette-smoking, beer-drinking, foul-mouthed, pot-bellied truck driver . . . well, that's not what I married, exactly. It was one of his incarnations. Later, he became a religious fanatic."

"He married you; you scared the hell out him. That how it goes?"

"Something like that," Maureen said.

"I met Bobby in college," she told him. "He was there on a football scholarship. Made the freshman team. Things were working out like they were supposed to. Bobby wasn't going to graduate magna cum laude, but he could squeeze by. He drank a little. Tried pot a couple of times. Quit because he thought it hurt his game.

"When it came to sex, Bobby was a gentleman. We didn't go all the way until late in our sophomore year. I didn't register for my junior year. Pregnant. He did the right thing. We got married. Of course it was the wrong thing. He became a truck driver. Just for awhile, he said, until he could figure things out. He never figured them out."

"What happened to the kid?" Shanahan asked.

"He died at thirteen, overdose. Our lives were going

to hell, anyway," Maureen said, her voice low in the darkness. He could barely hear her. "When Kevin died, we arrived."

"I'm sorry."

"Bobby blamed himself for Kevin's death, I'm sure of that. But he acted as if it were my fault. I already believed it was my fault. If I hadn't been working, maybe I could have picked up the trouble signs—you know. He rarely ate. Spent all his time in his room. I thought it was just teenage moodiness. That it would pass."

"Are you still blaming yourself?" Shanahan wanted to put his arms around her. He didn't.

"Not as much. Well, Bobby and I started drinking, started fighting. I had horrible headaches. Things were falling apart at work. A doctor gave me some tranquilizers. I liked them a lot. Being a zombie has its good side. At least that's what I thought. And between booze and drugs, I didn't feel a thing. I didn't argue anymore. Bobby had no fun in a rage by himself. He got brutal. I didn't give a shit."

"He hit you."

"I'd say it was a weekly thing. He'd feel worse, beg me to forgive him, swear he'd never do it again. Then he'd go on a binge, drink himself silly, go on a tear and I'd end up the punching bag."

"You left."

"No. He did, eventually. A funny thing happened, we got cable TV and Bobby started watching the TV preachers. That guy Swaggart, especially. Bobby stopped drinking. He stopped hitting me. He stopped getting angry, at least at me. One day, Swaggart came to town. At the Arena—you know, where the Pacers play basketball. And Bobby was born again."

"Sounds like an improvement," Shanahan said.

"You'd think so, wouldn't you? After that he wanted me to watch these preacher shows. I tried a couple of times. I tried to figure out what Bobby was getting from it. Then it hit. Swaggart was preaching hate. Bobby found a way to channel his hate. He found his religion. Hating drugs, hating alcohol, hating sex and hating me. It was natural, a way not to blame himself. Blame it on a conspiracy of Satan worshippers, homosexuals and pornographers. Sometimes, he'd include Democrats. He started reading the Bible. It was obsessive. Quoting from this and that, going through the Bible, like it was a grocery store, picking out the things he liked and putting them into his little shopping cart of sins.

"You know, one time, when he was angry with me, he screamed at me, calling me a 'secular humanist' like it was the most obscene thing he could think of. I couldn't help it. It was so funny, I laughed. Bobby . . . Bobby, what a silly name for a grown man. It fit though. That was the last time he hit me.

"During all this," Maureen continued, "I lost my job. It wasn't the bank's fault. They covered for me for a while, suggested counseling, but I was screwing up royally. I'd go on crying jags, that is, when I showed up for work. Finally they had enough. Bobby took his Bible and some clothes. For all I know, he's one of those guys passing the collection plate for Swaggart."

"You went on the skids?"

"I'm coming out of them, Shanahan. Bigger and better. I got religion, too, in a way. Only mine isn't based on hate. As I said before, I don't believe in suffering. I believe in happiness. Making people happy. Being happy. I don't know why yet, Shanahan, but you make me happy."

Shanahan rolled over to her, kissed her first on the cheek, then found her lips. His hands slowly moved from her cheek to her neck to her breasts. "I hope so. I want to."

Shanahan tried to imagine her son, what he looked like. He tried to imagine what his own son looked like. A lot of lost children, he thought. Then, all of a sudden, Shanahan wasn't thinking so clearly. Maureen saw to that.

———

It was barely morning. Night was just a thin gray line in the west. In the east, a pink light pushed forward a picture-postcard blue with basic movie-set fluffy clouds. The early dampness heightened the color. Kodachrome.

Casey was in good form, leaping to catch a high bounce, retrieving grounders like Shawon Dunston, waiting under a fly ball until it plopped into his open mouth. The exercise kept the dog trim, kept what flesh he had taut and muscular. After about the fortieth throw, Casey was panting hard and taking more time bringing the ball back to Shanahan. Finally, he dropped to the ground, let the ball roll out of his mouth between his two front legs and hyperventilated.

What day was it? Saturday. Perhaps he and Maureen could drive into the country, give the boys in the pale green, plain Buick parked out front a sightseeing tour of the hills in southern Indiana.

Not yet. It was imperative he stay a few steps ahead of Rafferty. The cops in Indianapolis weren't corrupt, at least by big-city standards. But the Republicans had been in charge for the last couple of decades and that was too long for any party. Too much of a chance for people to take their uncontested power and special interests for granted. They got the feeling they were governing by divine right. Rafferty was a smart cop, but not a good one. He wasn't the cop you used to see on *The Saturday Evening Post*'s covers by Norman Rockwell. Times change. Change or die. Even *The Saturday Evening Post* wasn't *The Saturday Evening Post* anymore. It died and a synthetic copy emerged at its resurrection.

Shanahan had to find Marquette. He had to contact Mrs. Stone. He also had to find a way to view those tapes.

He thought he remembered that Harmony, the guy with the computers, had a couple of VCRs. Maybe one of them was Beta. He couldn't call him because of the phone tap. He didn't want to get Harmony involved. That meant Shanahan had to find a way to lose that ugly Buick out front. He wanted to return the rented Lincoln, anyway.

He went inside and checked on Maureen. The room was warm. She had thrown back the top blanket and her nude body was amidst a swirl of sheets. She hadn't worked in a few days now. He wondered if she planned on staying at his place forever. He wasn't sure he minded.

In the kitchen, he wrote a short note, explaining that he and Casey were going to the store. As he walked by the ugly green Buick, he wished he'd had Casey's tennis ball with him. He could have tossed it in the open window and watched Casey leap through it, dropping sixty pounds of dog in their unsuspecting laps.

He passed the public phone booth. Shanahan wasn't sure just how savvy the cops were and went to the corner of the next block to the Village Pantry. Used to be a Mom and Pop's in the neighborhood, guys you knew by their first name. Now, there were these fluorescent boxes selling Doritos Tortilla Chips and Pepsi, operated by a teenager who wished he wasn't there and wished you weren't either.

"I wonder if I might use your phone," Shanahan asked the kid reading a comic book behind the case of glazed doughnuts.

"Sorry, it's a business phone. Company policy." He didn't even look up. "There's a phone booth down the street."

"For ten bucks, you wouldn't mind if I made a couple of local calls."

"How do I know they're local? You could be calling the Arabs."

"Count the beeps."

"Oh, yeah. Ten bucks?"

The kid shoved the phone over to him. Shanahan picked up the receiver then stopped before dialing. "You had this thing repaired lately? Anybody been in working on it?"

"No," the kid said, confused. "Doesn't it work?"

"By the way, when I leave here, a guy in a gray suit's going to come in and ask what I was doing in here. He'll pretend he's a cop, but he isn't. See, if you look real close at his badge you'll find the numbers are in the wrong place." What would the kid know about badge numbers?

"He's real crazy, so be careful, treat him real polite. I'm calling the asylum right now, they'll come and get him. When he asks about me, tell I'm just some weird guy you've seen in the neighborhood and that I spent twenty minutes trying to decide between whole wheat and white bread."

"No problem." The kid looked like he'd rather be serving time at the Marion County jail.

Shanahan dialed the time, pretending to talk to the director of a mental institution. He cupped his hand over the mouthpiece. "See what he's doing," Shanahan asked the kid, "but pretend you're straightening the Coke bottles in the window."

The kid did what he was told. Shanahan called Harmony, verified that he did have a Beta VCR. Shanahan asked if he could use it this afternoon. He could. Then he called Mrs. Stone to fill her in, with what little he could tell her. He wasn't going to tell her about the other woman just yet or about the change in the will and insurance.

Too late. She knew. The police had visited her at her sister's and all but arrested her on the spot. Apparently, Rafferty wanted to check his bag full of goodies before he threw her in jail.

"They believe I did it." She was very calm, the way some people react after a shock. "They say Will was dropping me from the insurance and canceling out my inheritance. Was he, Mr. Shanahan?"

"It appears that way."

"Then why didn't you tell me?" Shanahan thought he could detect cool anger in her calmness.

"I didn't want to tell you until I was sure who this other person was. Did they tell you who Mr. Stone was putting in his will?"

"They mentioned a name, but I didn't recognize it. Lieutenant Rafferty said it probably was, as he put it, my husband's bastard son. They're looking for the woman. I really don't think my husband was all that interested in women. They wanted me to confess. They said they would go a lot easier on me if I'd confess." Her voice was tiny. "You're supposed to be helping me, Mr. Shanahan."

"I'm trying, that is if you still want me to."

"I've gone this far with you. Please, just hurry and get this thing over with."

"I need your help."

"Mine?"

"In half an hour, I want you to call me at home. I want you to tell me I'm fired."

"But I just told . . ."

"Listen, Mrs. Stone. My phone is tapped and I'd like them to think I'm off the case. Tell them your sister has advised you to get an attorney and to stop messing around with a third-rate over-the-hill detective."

Mrs. Stone laughed. "You really want me to say that?"

"Get really nasty, if you like."

"I used to act, you know, in college. *Cat on a Hot Tin Roof.* I was pretty wonderful. That's what I need, a little fun." She laughed again and Shanahan started liking her a lot, though he had a hard time imagining her in a steamy drama. He liked her, but could he ever like Rafferty? Maybe. After he punched his lights out.

"They're burying him today," she said almost as an afterthought.

"I know. I'll be there."

"But I'm about to fire you."

"I know. You won't see me. Bye."

Shanahan pulled the clerk aside. "Whatever you do, don't tell him I made a phone call. That will rile him something fierce."

Outside, Shanahan waved at the guy in the gray suit. "You ought to get some coffee and doughnuts. Good doughnuts, help keep your energy up." He handed the cop a napkin.

———

Maureen was in the kitchen, fixing coffee, still drowsy and dreamy eyed.

"How 'bout I whip up some eggs, potatoes, bacon and whole wheat toast?" Shanahan asked.

"You seem pretty chipper."

"I haven't had so much fun since little Eddie Blevins got his weenie caught in a milk of magnesia bottle."

"I take it you didn't like little Eddie what's his name?"

The phone rang.

"Some day I'll tell you about little Eddie Blevins," he said, picking up the receiver.

"This is Mrs. Stone, Mr. Shanahan."

"I don't think we should discuss anything on the phone, Mrs.—"

She cut him off. "There's very little to discuss. That's precisely why I'm calling. I'm afraid I'm going to have to dismiss you."

"Mrs. Stone—"

"I've been advised to get a lawyer and let him handle my affairs. Under the circumstances, I think it's good advice."

"What circumstances?"

"Mr. Shanahan, I'm sure you don't want me to go into all that. Consider yourself fortunate you'll be receiving a check for your time and expenses as soon as you present your bill."

"Mrs. Stone . . ."

"Is there really anything else that needs to be said?" She hadn't gotten angry. She underplayed it all the way and it was good, real good. So good, he wondered just how good an actress she really was.

"No, I guess not."

━━━

Shanahan took his breakfast to the sofa by the window, peering out through the slats of the venetian blinds. Maureen sat beside him, resting the plate on one bare knee.

"What's happening?" she asked.

"Nothing at the moment." Shanahan looked down at the green Buick. He finished his breakfast. Maureen warmed up his coffee. Finally, the unmarked car drove off. It passed by the house slowly, the cop staring at the house, then picked up speed and disappeared.

Shanahan went to the bathroom, turned on the shower and stepped out of his clothes. The small, tiled room filled with steam. He stepped in, let the hot water rush over him. He let his mind run across the feeble list of suspects: an unknown burglar, Kessler, Mrs. Stone and the "other woman."

"Is there room for two?" It was Maureen's voice. He could tell the shower curtain had opened by the brief blast of cool air. Then, he felt arms around his waist. "I like it steamy," she said.

"My God, Maureen, I really don't think I can keep up with you."

"Oh, really," she said, her hands sliding down, proving him wrong.

———

At the cemetery, Shanahan stood on a hill nearly a half mile from the grave site. Slowly, he scanned the small crowd through his binoculars. A minister. Rafferty. Mrs. Stone. Olivia. He couldn't see their faces, only their backs as the mechanical device lowered the coffin. No relatives? No friends? How low-key could it get? Olivia helped Mrs. Stone into the long black limousine.

Not many men get two graves, Shanahan thought. The first one haphazardly dug in his own backyard. Either the murderer was in a hurry, too exhausted or weak to finish the job, or maybe interrupted. Or possibly the murderer wanted the body found quickly, but didn't want to be too obvious about it. After all, something to add a little weight to the corpse, what with the water company's reservoir a few feet away, they would never have found him. Less risky, too.

Shanahan walked down the hill. He looked at the grave, and then started walking back to his car. He had parked outside the main gate on a small sidestreet. Did the gravestones, the size of them, measure the amount of grief, guilt or simply wealth? Shanahan wouldn't be buried here, if he could help it. He had left strict instructions to be incinerated. If it weren't for a powerful mortician's lobby, he'd instruct them to put his ashes in a trash bag and leave it out front of his house on Wednesday morning.

Pretty place, though, the graveyard. Quiet. A few stone angels were falling apart from the acid rain. So much for mankind's stab at permanence. Immortality.

10

Shanahan liked these kinds of days. Almost no humidity. Shadows fell softly in the sun, dappled sunlight dropped through the trees on the streets. Even Fountain Square seemed cheery.

Harmony also seemed in good spirits, but then it was Shanahan's guess that Harmony was indeed harmonious. Balanced. Harry's granddaughter was a lucky girl. The young man, dressed in what appeared to be his usual loose cotton pants and shirt, welcomed him with an offer of lemonade, then showed him the VCR and how to operate it.

Shanahan wasn't sure what to expect. He thought he'd find something implying blackmail. Some grainy, badly lit pictures of a man and woman in a sleazy hotel, somebody taking a payoff or the camera as witness to some other crime. He was, however, surprised at what he found. Five minutes through the tape, he aimed the little metal box at the VCR and the screen clicked to gray. Shanahan leaned back, trying to figure out what he saw and what the significance might be.

The video started out like a low-budget teen film. Innocent enough. After the credits, a couple of young guys played basketball. They joked, generally screwed around. The sound was bad and the camera wasn't real steady. Not Hollywood standards, not TV standards, but better than most amateurs making a video album for the family.

The scene cut away to the locker room. Some post-adolescent banter. Then a hand moved to a crotch and within a few seconds, one guy's gym shorts were down around his ankles and the other guy was down on his knees tending to business.

It looked like Stone was gay, kept the cassette in his safe so Mrs. Stone wouldn't discover it. But it didn't fit in with Shanahan's theory about the other woman. He'd have to watch the rest of the video, but now he moved onto the other video cassette. Maybe it would hold a more obvious key to the puzzle.

The second video was short. It had no credits and was shot even more amateurishly than the first. And Shanahan watched all of it, though it wasn't exactly his cup of tea. Two things fascinated Shanahan. One, the naked black guy lying on the bed, moving with a kind of seductive grace, looked familiar. He had seen the face recently, somewhere. Shanahan wasn't sure where or when.

The second thing that struck Shanahan was the bed the guy was on. It was Stone's. Stone wasn't in the video, but his bed definitely was. Stone, no doubt, was holding the camera. Shanahan put the video in reverse, stopped, froze action on a close-up of the guy's face. He studied the face, letting it make a deep, unforgettable impression.

Shanahan rewound the tape, ejected it and put the other tape back in. The locker-room scene lasted maybe ten minutes, it was followed by another male sex fantasy, then another. Shanahan was beginning to think it was just an entertainment for Stone, when he recognized the black guy, the one on Stone's bed. The guy was younger . . . but it was the same guy.

Shanahan reversed the video, started that section over. He didn't know what he was looking for, but now he wanted to see the details. A nearly bare apartment, shot in available light. A Jimi Hendrix poster on the wall. A stereo in a corner. The bay window had no curtains or shades. Out the window, Shanahan could make out a hill. He backed it up, froze the frame on the window. He was pretty sure the video had been shot in San Francisco.

It made sense, sort of. The earlier letters to Stone were from San Francisco. The later ones were local. Could this be Marquette? Could the letters have been written by Marquette? Maybe there was no "other woman," just an "other" man. Mrs. Stone had alluded to that earlier, hadn't she? She said she wasn't sure Stone was interested in women. Shanahan had let that pass. Did she know more than she was telling?

Shanahan watched the rest of the video, speeding through most of it, looking for the reappearance of the black guy. At one point, Harmony came over to fill up Shanahan's hardly touched lemonade glass.

"Is this part of the case?" Harmony asked.

Shanahan laughed, knowing what was going through Harmony's mind.

"Well, you never know," Harmony laughed, realizing the inference. "It's okay by me, whatever gets you through the night."

Then suddenly he gasped. "Christ!"

Shanahan looked up at Harmony, whose eyes were locked on the video screen.

"That looks painful," Harmony said, shaking his head to break the spell, then returned to his mass of cables, monitors, computers, printers and cameras.

Shanahan reran the short video. One more time. He didn't know what he was looking for. And he didn't know what he found when he found it. Between scenes, there was a quick flash of something. It was almost subliminal. Using the freeze-frame button, Shanahan moved until he could see what it was. Numbers. Three sets of numbers, one between each scene. He took out his notebook, copied them down.

The tan Malibu pulled into the driveway. Shanahan was tired. He leaned back in his seat, feeling slightly nauseous. It wasn't from looking at that stuff on the video, though he might have enjoyed himself more had there been women in them. Maybe, it was more a strange kind of exhaustion. Sadness of the mind, maybe, rather than of the heart. A man like Stone felt the need to lock his little secret in a safe. A man so frightened of his own nature that he coveted little snippets of people's intimate lives and denied any intimacy in his own. Then, who was Shanahan to judge?

The black guy was Marquette. Had to be. The kid's face, those eyes were saying "You can have me. Why don't you just love me? Why the distance?" Shanahan could picture Stone, camera on his shoulder, standing at the end of the bed. He remembered that part of the letter that said, "It's true I've slept with other people. Sometimes a person needs the warmth of another body to stay alive."

Shanahan suddenly wanted to find someone whose life was going right. The chance of that happening soon seemed unlikely. He was pretty sure he had to find Marquette. Unfortunately, he was pretty sure Marquette's life wasn't going right either.

Would it do Shanahan any good to call San Francisco to find Marquette's family? Hell, most people in San Francisco aren't from San Francisco and Marquette's family probably wasn't there either.

He gave it a shot though. Went to the library, carefully copied the phone numbers from the huge Bay Area phone book. He called. There were a few with no answer. He'd check them later. Otherwise nothing.

Back in his own driveway, Shanahan finally worked up the energy to get out of the car. He picked up a stack of envelopes and a magazine in the mailbox. Normally, finding a new copy of *Horticulture* was a real treat. Today, it wasn't. He sorted through the envelopes. One was from a retirement community. Another, addressed to Mrs. Dieter Shanahan, said she'd won a prize. All she would have to do was drive 150 miles to a new resort and she'd win a new Pontiac, a mink coat or an electric skillet. Guaranteed. No obligation. He used to get interesting junk mail. Now they all had something to do with his actuarial proximity to death. "Thanks, guys."

———

In the afternoon, in the quiet of his garden, he ran through the computer print outs. Could be that Stone paid the rent on this guy's apartment. He found a debit for $375 dated near the end of each month during the last year and earlier $350 a month to the same people. The code was BRAD. PROP. Sounded like a rent check to him.

The Yellow Pages showed a listing for Bradenton Properties, Inc. On the next page, there was an ad for Bradenton, twelve apartment houses, all near downtown. He'd call, but first he wanted to check in with Rafferty. Tell him he was off the case as if Rafferty didn't know. What he really wanted to know was if Mrs. Stone was still their number-one patsy.

"Indianapolis Police Department, will you hold please?"

Shanahan shook his head and paced with the phone, then noticed the note on his desk. Great detective he was. He'd been using the phone for more than an hour and this was the first time he saw the note.

> Gone a couple of days. Want to give us both a breather. Will call tonight, just to say hi. As always.

It was signed "The Pushy Broad."

"May I help you?"

"Homicide please," Shanahan said, then heard a

series of clicks, wondering if he was on his way to the usual disconnection. Police departments usually ran a decade or two behind everyday technology.

"Homicide," came a bored male voice.

"Lieutenant Rafferty." He waited to hear more clicks.

"I'm sorry, sir," the voice said, not sorry at all, "but Lieutenant Rafferty's not in homicide."

"Since when?"

The guy wasn't in the mood for conversation. "Do you want Lieutenant Rafferty or do you want homicide?"

"Give me Gamble," Shanahan said on impulse.

"Right." Click, click, click.

"Homicide. Sergeant Gamble."

"Congratulations on making sarge," Shanahan said.

"You know the Titanic went down, don't ya? I made sergeant five years ago. So who the hell's this, Rip Van Winkle?"

"Shanahan. Sorry, I must have missed the headlines. Everybody's changing. Rafferty's not in homicide and you are. I still think of you as a vice cop."

"How am I supposed to take that? Doesn't matter. Didn't I tell you I made sergeant down there at Delaney's? Tell you the truth, it's kind of embarrassing. Sergeant ain't much when you been bustin' your ever lovin' ass for more than forty years. Say, I forgot to tell you I ran into Schmidt the other day. Quit the force a few years ago. Started his own security business. The bastard sold it for a couple of mil. Now the fucker's off to the Caribbean. Got himself a dolly, a couple of centuries younger than he is and not a care in the world."

"Speaking of old times"—Shanahan winced. He didn't give a shit about old times—"what's Rafferty doing these days?"

"You mean when he's not polishing somebody's rear? Well, you ought to know what he's doing. I understand you're the hired nose on the Stone case, then I understand suddenly you aren't."

"Yeah. Ran into Rafferty. Assumed he was in homicide."

"You know what assumptions are, don't you buddy?"

"Whatever you do, don't tell me."

"Rafferty's in special projects."

"What the hell is that?"

"It's a new fangled word here at IPD, which means we're doing something and we don't want anybody to know what it is because there's a good chance we don't either."

"Great," Shanahan said.

"Best I can make out, there's two ways you get into special projects. First, the department don't know what else to do with you. . . ."

"Or?"

"Like I said, they don't want anybody to know what you're up to. In the case of Rafferty, it's a toss up. He rides the political roller coasters around here like he's got a free pass to Disneyland. One day his name don't mean jackshit. The next day the chief is guarding his chair 'cause he thinks Rafferty's making a run at his job. You tell me."

"Why would he be working on the Stone murder? Murder is usually considered homicide, or is there some distinction I don't know about?"

"Oh . . ."

Shanahan could almost see Gamble settling back in his chair, getting comfortable, sipping a cup of cold coffee and sucking on one of his skinny, rum-soaked cigars.

"Big shot, man with heavy connections to the city dads gets iced in his own backyard. They don't want some hard-nosed cop like me screwing up IPD's public affairs image. You know, being a professional doesn't mean knowing what you're doing anymore. It means wearing the right clothes and talking like Kissinger. So they get a slippery-tongued phony like Rafferty to calm down the nervous nellies at the Chamber of Commerce and to stick it to the press so nice the press don't know they've been stuck."

"Are they going to make an arrest?" Shanahan asked.

"Thought you were off it."

"Idle curiosity."

"Sure," Gamble said, "You've met my mom, Mother Theresa? You don't give up on anything. Don't let Rafferty know you're still poking around. He's got a hard-on for you and he doesn't believe in kissing you first."

"I won't tell, if you won't," Shanahan said.

"They're still going after Stone's old lady."

"Why are they waiting? The last thing Rafferty told me was they had the motive, the body and the weapon."

"Prosecutor says 'leave no stone unturned.'" Gamble laughed. "This case has to be tight as a newborn's ass, Shanahan. The old lady is so loaded she could buy her own law firm. So they're going over her house like it was Tutankhamen's grave."

"Not if her money is all tied up in the estate."

"It ain't, Shanahan. I'd think you rent-a-cops would know more about the people who hire you. She had more money than he did. Family money. The Benson family. Quiet money. Money that talks softly but carries a big stick. Hell, even their private foundations have private foundations. Ring a bell?"

"Yeah," Shanahan said, feeling like a fool.

"You should be ashamed."

"How do you know all this."

"Keep my eyes open. Count the cards as they're played, pal, and you'll learn who holds trump."

"But that screws up her motive, doesn't it? She had so much money, why would she kill him simply because she was written out of his will?"

"Woman scorned, maybe. Who the hell knows?

Maybe he was dicking around with another broad. Or could be greed. You know those rich folks. They get addicted. They just gotta have more."

"Thanks."

"Listen, Shanahan. Rafferty's got a lot of trump, and hearts ain't his long suit."

"Thanks," Shanahan said again, grateful for Gamble's concern.

"Sure. Keep me in the loop on this thing. Buy me a beer someday, will ya', Shanahan?"

"I will."

Shanahan pushed down the button on the phone, then dialed. He was lucky to find the Bradenton Property rental office open on Saturday. He used his TV repairman routine.

"When they gave me the order," Shanahan told the lady, "somebody had spilled coffee all over it. Couldn't read the address and phone number, but they did remember the last name and that the guy lived in a Bradenton Property." It was the best line he could come up with.

"That's funny, why would . . ."

"And he's going to be real upset if we don't fix his TV."

"I'll be a minute." Shanahan got an earful of Muzak and decided he liked the kind Harmony played. The music cut out and the voice returned. "I'm sorry, I don't have a Marquette."

"How about a Stone? Maybe the name was Marguerite Stone. I mean, you just can't read this damn thing."

He waited, thinking he recognized a song, but then on Muzak, Cab Calloway sounded like Elvis Presley.

"I've got a Juanita Stone and a Beverly Stone, but no Marguerite."

"Maybe you know who I'm talking about. Black guy, slender . . ."

"Listen, we have over eight hundred apartments.

There's no way . . . how do you know what he looks like?"

"Oops." Shanahan hung up.

——

Shanahan checked the mail boxes at each apartment house. No fun. No success. He even talked with Juanita and Beverly Stone. Juanita was an ancient woman who was confused by Shanahan's presence at her front door.

"My dear, you've found him," she said before Shanahan could explain. She had a small, weak voice that trilled with excitement. Shanahan knew she didn't mean Marquette.

"No, I'm sorry . . ."

"He's dead isn't he?" Her face went dark. "I should never have opened the window, but I thought they were all in." Over the lady's shoulder, Shanahan could see maybe twenty-five bird cages and maybe twice the number of parakeets. "It's my fault," she said.

"I haven't seen him," he told the lady. "It's warm outside. He'll be all right. Don't worry." She was already lost in her thoughts and shut the door.

Beverly Stone was younger, maybe fifty, and cranky. She looked at Shanahan as if he was a cockroach in the silverware drawer. No connection here. Nothing.

——

It was six-thirty when he got home. The first thing he thought about was dinner. He had managed to forget food all day. He put some vermicelli on to boil. He'd eat alone tonight. First time in four days. Seemed strange.

Then he dialed Harmony. "I didn't think you'd be there."

"I'm always here. I work here. I live here," Harmony said. "I'll die here, slumped over the discs, my soul on the way up to pixel heaven."

"I need a favor."

"You're my most interesting client. Why not?"

"Those cassettes. Can you get a photograph off of it? Something I can carry around?"

"Sure. Freeze the video image and shoot it."

"Can you do it quick, like tonight?" Shanahan didn't like screwing up somebody's Saturday night.

"I've got an old four-by-five press camera with a Polaroid attachment."

"Does that mean yes?"

"Yes. Take me only a few minutes. Is that all?"

"Yeah," Shanahan said, then remembered. "No . . . I need to know where gay people hang out these days."

"Don't let my long hair fool you," Harmony said.

"C'mon, I've been in cold storage for the last decade, but I used to know the names of a couple of places."

"Actually, there is a place. Melissa and I went to a disco a couple of years ago. Supposed to be the hottest place in town and gay. We had a good time considering I hate disco. The place is called Talbot Street. It's been a couple of years though."

"Where is it?"

"Talbot Street, like the name says, near Twenty-second. Used to be the Black Curtain Theater."

Shanahan knew the place.

11

Shanahan leaned against the kitchen counter, eating his bowl of vermicelli spiced with garlic, onion and melted butter. He was trying to decide whether to call it a day or shower, pick up the Polaroid at Harmony's and venture into the night. He wasn't thrilled about spending a night in gay bars. He was rarely in a festive mood.

What was the choice? Maureen wasn't going to show up. If he stayed home, he'd just hang around with the ghost of Elaine and feel sorry for her, or himself, or both. If he went to Delaney's, Harry would be full of it and full of embarrassing questions, after which Shanahan would drink himself into anger or a self-pitying stupor. It was a hell of a multiple choice.

It was nine-thirty when he left Harmony's with a remarkably good likeness of Marquette, and now he sat behind the wheel of his tan Malibu parked in the potholed lot across from Talbot Street.

He got out of the car, locked it and crossed the street. The problem was that the place on Talbot Street wasn't called Talbot Street anymore. Changed hands and, apparently, clientele. The man at the door, a handsomely attired black gentleman of indeterminate age, pointed down the dark street to a bit of neon glowing on the side of a corner building and told him he'd find what he wanted there.

"The bowling alley?" Shanahan asked, remembering the neighborhood of twenty years ago.

"Not a bowling alley, man. A strolling alley, where boys will be girls, where the curls ain't real and that's the deal, my man."

He walked the dimly lit block, noticing most of the

houses were boarded up. Decent old houses, deserted now with gray, raw wood peeking out from behind tattered ribbons of paint. Everything reminded him of death and decay.

The sign said, Two Picture I.D.s, but the kid behind the counter took Shanahan's two-dollar cover and didn't ask for proof he was twenty-one. The kid reached for a rubber stamp and applied it on the back of Shanahan's right hand. You could see the date under the black light, but it disappeared as Shanahan moved down the narrow hall.

He passed a door that led into a small bar. Three or four people were leaning over the bar talking to the guy behind it. Shanahan kept going, moving toward the sound of the music. To the right was a coat checkroom. To his left were photographs of the performers. Drag queens, surprisingly attractive in a black-and-white glossy sort of way. Below the photographs were such names as Chelsea Pearl, Blanche Dubois, Amanda Del Rio, and Lanora Taki. And below the names were stacks of literature—several pamphlets on AIDS and a newspaper called *The Body Works*. He picked up a copy, rolled it up and stuck it in his jacket pocket.

The main room of the bar was huge. Between seventy-five and a hundred tables with tablecloths, ashtrays and little red brandy-snifter-type candles with plastic netting. One set of tables was raised above the dance floor and a mirrored ball spun lights out over the nearly empty room. Behind the dance floor was a stage. Directly across from the stage was a sound and light booth. Along one wall was one helluva bar. There were at least four TV monitors, strategically placed in the room.

"Big place, no people," Shanahan said to the bartender.

"About an hour, they start coming in," said the

bartender. "And an hour after that, you won't be able to move. Can I get you something?"

"A Miller and some information."

"Oooookay!" the bartender said, going over to the aluminum sliding doors and pulling out a can of beer. "But if you want a table, we're sold out."

Shanahan turned, looked out over a sea of empty tables, each with a sign saying Reserved.

The bartender delivered the beer. "Glass?"

"Please," Shanahan said. He didn't mind drinking out of a bottle, but he hated aluminum. "I don't need a table, thanks."

The bartender came back with a plastic cup.

"You're not interested in Mr. Gay Texas and the runner-up to Miss Gay America?" The bartender smiled.

"Not tonight." Shanahan drank his beer from the can.

"Didn't think so. What kind of information are you looking for?"

Shanahan pulled out the photograph of Marquette. "Have you seen him before?"

The guy looked at it for a couple of seconds. "No. I might have seen him, then again I might not. He could have stopped in a few times, but he's not a regular."

"Would you know more about him if I left a substantial tip?"

"Wish I could say yes. But I can't." The bartender, a handsome fellow in a rough sort of way, was good-natured, apparently used to strange requests. "You're not a cop. And you're not his dad. Why are you interested?"

"A friend of his died recently. Thought he ought to know."

"I'm sorry. Wish I could help you. Have you checked the other bars?"

"Not yet." Shanahan took a deep swallow of his beer, put the half-empty can on the bar along with two dollars and left. There was a line of people at the door, waiting to pay the cover and get their hands stamped. A guy well over six foot, wearing a red beaded gown and sporting a monstrous beehive, stood behind the money taker kibitzing with the crowd.

"Where you going, honey?" the guy asked.

"Hell," Shanahan said.

"You goin' in the wrong direction."

"Lay off, will ya?" asked the guy with the dollar bills. "You're scaring off the clientele."

"Honey, I put the ugh in uglee. Bye, babee," the behive called after Shanahan.

———

The newspaper provided more leads than he really wanted. He'd already hit five bars. Shanahan, sitting in his Malibu with the overhead light on, disregarded the people moving into the club across the street. Instead, he plotted out his evening, wondering if he could make all fifteen gay bars. Fortunately, they were all within a few miles of each other, huddled in the old industrial section. What they held in common were streets empty of traffic during the night, places that wouldn't draw the curious, places where the identities of those who entered and left would not be noticed.

It was quarter of two when he arrived at the last place on his list of bars. Like the others, it was hard to find. No neon sign blasting out into the night. A light over the door of an old house and the address. Shanahan could hear the music as he approached the door. He took a deep breath before opening it.

It was a small place, with a crowd a decade or two older than the ones that frequented the dance bars. He edged in and leaned against the wall, close to the door. He figured he owed himself a beer. Other than the sip or two he had gulped down at the drag bar, he had merely gone in, asked his questions and left. No one knew Marquette.

No one could even remember seeing him. Not the slightest glimmer of recognition.

Shanahan looked up, over the heads of the crowd. A couple of guys were on a makeshift stage, taking their clothes off to the music. Half the crowd watched the gyrations. Shanahan watched the crowd. He had already seen a cross section of the gay-bar patrons. Nothing extraordinary. Nothing shocking.

There was a country-and-western bar and restaurant, where sad faces listened to sad songs, a yuppie bar where lean guys in polo shirts seemed to be engaged in good-natured gossip. He'd found a couple of more earthy bars, guys in Levi's and leather hanging around the pool tables. In most cases, Shanahan wouldn't have guessed they were gay, save for the absence of women and the occasional displays of male-to-male affection.

He wasn't as uncomfortable as he thought he'd be. He inched his way between two guys at the bar, ordered a Miller and relaxed back against the wall and watched the boys in the G-strings play the tables, undulating hips teasing the guys at the tables until they couldn't resist stuffing some green in the little triangle of fabric.

This world wasn't so different. It was a mirror of the straight bars where "Girls" hustled tips, and twirled tit tassels. And if he had understood anything new this evening, it was that the society was mirrored. For the thousands of gay men he saw this evening, there were probably at least that many or more living the quiet life. Sitting home, watching television, having dinner, going to the movies. And that could be what Marquette was about. Except for one thing: In Marquette's letter, he said he had slept with other people. You don't do that in a vacuum. There had to be other ways to meet than the bars.

One of the guys sitting at the bar had had enough and shoved his way toward the door. Shanahan angled for the seat. He arrived just in time to get an eyeful of ass. One of the dancers had climbed on the bar and moved in on Shanahan. The guy bent over, head upside down, looking at Shanahan from between his spread legs.

"You having fun yet?" the kid asked.

Shanahan had to laugh. Cute ass, but what would he do with the rest of him?

The guy turned, lowered himself down in front of Shanahan, whose face was now a couple of inches from a leather-covered crotch. Shanahan took a dollar from his change at the bar and handed it to the kid. Once the dancer got the money, he moved on quickly.

The noise was getting to Shanahan. He was exhausted by the accumulation of loud sounds, sounds that made no sense to him. The lyrics might as well have been Japanese. He could only recognize the relentless bass beat of the drums.

The sound stopped abruptly and the dancers scampered off the floor. The DJ had turned down the volume and was making an announcement. "Fuzzy navels, anyone?" Shanahan took the moment of quiet to ask the bartender about Marquette. The guy shrugged, shook his head.

Either the lights dimmed or Shanahan was about to pass out. Fortunately, the lights came up on the stage to the sound of excited applause. Some of the crowd stood up, blasting out the sheer whistling sounds you hear at wrestling matches. A kid stepped up on stage, no more than eighteen, wearing blue jeans, a Levi's jacket and a cowboy hat made of straw. His smile seemed to light up the room and the applause increased again. He danced, looking around the room, his eyes stopping briefly here and there at what Shanahan presumed were familiar faces. Unlike the other dancers, this kid moved with a sort of seductive grace. Fluid. Not effeminate, but like an athlete. Also, unlike the others, this dancer had the full attention of the crowd.

Four or five of the other dancers came out to watch him. Shanahan wanted to leave. He didn't. He had one more question. What about male prostitutes? He figured maybe these guys took on a little action on the side. Even if they didn't, there had to be a place to go to buy sex. There had to be a demand. And where there's demand, there's supply.

And if Marquette had been so much in love with Stone and just wanted a warm body without the complications of a relationship, then maybe, just maybe Marquette was willing to pay for an unfettered night of companionship. There were certainly periods in Shanahan's life when buying a body was a tantalizing idea. A couple of times, it had been more than speculation.

Shanahan couldn't get the bartender's attention. He, like the others, was mesmerized by the show the kid was putting on. Shanahan waited. The second number, brought on by a loud standing ovation, was the big number. This all-American, college-freshman-style kid was down to a small G-string and guys waited in line for the chance to touch him.

Shanahan tried to picture the kid's parents, sitting there watching him perform, wondering where they'd gone wrong, wondering what would become of him. Or did they care? The real question, though, was where did this guy learn to do what he did? The look was innocent. But the way the kid's hands swept up the thighs and caressed the crotch wasn't. He was in control and played to the prurient fantasy interests of the crowd with masterful strokes.

Once the line died down, the kid, still in his hat but giving every appearance he was going to remove his G-string, moved from table to table, pausing, suggesting, avoiding all hands that didn't have money in them and jutting his hips forward slowly, invitingly, when they did. In moments, the dancer was beside Shanahan. His eyes locked on Shanahan's. Shanahan handed him a dollar. The kid looked surprised, but didn't move away. Instead, he gave Shanahan a childish peck on the cheek as if saying thanks for not trying to cop a feel.

Shanahan could feel the heat, the blood rushing to his face. He looked around foolishly to see who might have seen. What? He regretted his instincts. The dancer looked hurt, gave a small smile and whirled back into the crowd.

Shanahan had to get out of there. However, there was a crowd at the door, necks straining to get a glimpse of the kid in the straw hat, waiting to get in.

The bartender came over, asked Shanahan if he wanted another drink.

Shanahan nodded, "Wait a minute," he told the bartender, "if a guy is from out of town and wanted to find somebody to"—he could barely form the word—"you know, a . . ."

"Hustler?" the bartender filled in the blank.

"Yeah."

"I wouldn't know." Of course he knew. Just too damned many questions from a stranger.

"Worshington Shtreet," came the slurred speech of the man sitting next to him, having trouble crushing his cigarette out in the ashtray.

"Washington Street? Where on Washington Street?"

"Easht, 'bout Shtate Shtreet on out?"

"When?"

"When?" The guy took another sip of beer, turned to Shanahan, trying to focus and looking puzzled.

"What time? Late afternoon? Evening? What days? When?" Shanahan was impatient.

"Kind of a hurry, aren't cha, fella?"

"Yeah, in a hurry. Well?"

The guy looked around as if he were going to find the answer on the wall somewhere.

"I spect jush about anytime you want?" The guy

looked at Shanahan like he was an idiot for not knowing.

Shanahan would investigate another time. The night had been too long.

———

In the dark of his room, Shanahan could hear everything. Car doors slamming two blocks away, leaves fluttering against the screen, a motorcycle revving in the distance and the rustling of night animals in his garden. There was another sound. Closer.

At first, it was just a strange sound that kept Shanahan awake. He couldn't locate it in the dark of his bedroom, though he didn't stir, head on the pillow, controlling his breathing. His body was tired, but his mind raced.

Finally, he turned to find a moth flapping, stupidly banging itself against the cool blue light of his digital clock-radio: 3:25 a.m.

At 4:30 a.m., he heard breathing. Not his own. It was outside. Casey hadn't stirred. Perhaps the wind blew the scent away. He slipped his .45 from the drawer and walked naked to the window. He squinted out into the darkness. All he could see were shades of black, darker where the trees were, lighter at the sky.

He paused. It was breathing he heard, unless he was going crazy. Not just one set of breaths but two, maybe three. The sounds were near, just a few feet away. He could almost smell the warmth. He walked quietly and quickly to the kitchen, found the flashlight and returned to the living room, where there was a window at an angle to the bedroom.

He looked again into the darkness. The sounds seemed to come from the roof, directly above the bedroom window. The hair on the back of his neck bristled. The gun in one hand and the flashlight in the other, he aimed both in the direction of the breathing and flashed on the light.

In that flash, everything from the silly to the sublime went through his mind. Everything from angels to aliens. He doubted his sanity. He wondered if he were dreaming. The beam caught a large pair of green eyes, then another pair, then a third, all belonging to a matched set of racoons.

He went back to bed. The adrenaline would take hours to dissipate. Shanahan shoved both pillows against the headboard, sat up in bed, stared dumbly into the darkness. Everything seemed so fucking hopeless.

Shanahan didn't notice sleep overtake him. He dreamed. Partially covered by fall leaves, he was sleeping in his garden. As he breathed out, swarms of brown moths fluttered from his chest. Then, he awoke wondering if it was a premonition. He was old enough for death to steal him away as he slept.

He longed for Maureen. He wanted to hold her, hold on to her, prevent himself from slipping away.

12

Sunday morning. In the garden, Shanahan reassured himself it was not yet autumn, that the dream was probably not an early death advisory. The peonies were about to open. He felt better.

It was early, yet heat was already in the air. He looked up at the silver maple, leaves turned inward. That meant it would rain sometime today. That would clear the moisture in the air and dowse his garden.   DOUSE

Shanahan went inside, reread Maureen's note. She said she'd be "gone a couple of days." How long was a couple of days? And why didn't she call last night? She probably did. So what did that mean? If she called and got no answer all night long, would she bother to call again or take it as Shanahan's way of dumping her? Why didn't he have an answering machine? All normal P.I.'s have answering machines.

He called the massage parlor. Surprisingly, there was an answer. Apparently Saturday night stretched well into the morning. The woman who answered wasn't happy.

"The bitch never even bothered to call. Here two goddamn weeks and pulls out without so much as a 'kiss my ass.'"

Shanahan slumped into the chair, stomach sinking rapidly. Then he remembered her driver's license. There was an address. Could he remember it? He pictured her face, the usual unflattering photo with Maureen J. Smith's head and shoulders in front of a blue screen. The birthdate was 12-12-44. The address was 2035 N. Drexel.

The house was a little white frame bungalow on a street of frame bungalows, all built at the same time and probably by the same builder. It was one of the first of the post–World War II tract housing developments.

Shanahan could hear his car crush the gravel in the drive. Her car was gone and there was something deadly quiet about the house. He went up on the small porch, knocked. No answer. He tried looking through the window. The venetian blinds were closed. He went around to the side windows, then to the back. Every view was shut off.

He jiggled the knob at the back door. It wouldn't budge. He went back to his car, opened the trunk, fumbled with the spare tire and found his little pack of breaking-and-entering tools. He was rusty. It took him a couple of minutes to manipulate the lock. Inside it was hot, stuffy and very empty. Even the corners had been swept clean and the trash removed. Whoever cleaned it out didn't even leave a wire coat hanger.

On his way back to the car, he checked the porch. No Sunday paper on the doorstep. The mailbox was empty and there was a small cobweb covering the top.

At noon, Shanahan set out to find a male hustler. It was his last best hope of finding Marquette. Shanahan felt uneasy about it. What if he got the wrong one, some born-again Baptist's kid? He'd have to be careful.

Shanahan's Malibu cruised east on Washington Street, from near downtown, then out as far as Arlington. Almost six miles. Nothing he could see resembled a kid on the make. A few down and outers crashing into sobriety, a couple of kids on the monkey bars in the park. Used car lots, lots of used car lots, full of Detroit dinosaurs and repossessed Camaros. Used appliance stores, interspersed with some run-down bars. This was a dirty, gray part of the city.

The only color relief—and that wasn't saying much—were the new fast-food shops: the Taco Bell and Church's Fried Chicken places. More than anything, they added to the desolation.

Shanahan repeated his search twice, then pressed on the gas, car now heading west until he had passed through downtown, through great swatches of land scraped clean by huge bulldozers and cranes, all being cleared for the new 125-acre state park, zoo, Western art museum, hotel and some piece of architecture that would be the city's version of the Eiffel Tower. He drove farther west until the neighborhoods mirrored the one he had left on the east side. More boarded up buildings, more used car lots, adult bookstores and then the area of "Adult Relaxation Centers."

He stopped where Maureen worked. It wasn't the same lady at the desk. This one seemed pleasant enough until he asked for Maureen.

"She's not here today," she said as if she'd just swallowed something nasty. "But," she said full of hope, "we have other lovely girls." She stood up, about to lead him into the next room. She was plain, not an unattractive woman, yet obviously not there to compete.

"No, you see I'm looking for Maureen."

"I'm afraid I can't help you there."

"I'm her father," Shanahan said. "Just got in from South Bend and I stopped by her house, but she doesn't live there anymore."

The lady raised an eyebrow as if to say "so who's surprised?" She turned, headed back to her desk. "I wish I could help, but I'm afraid I just don't know. . . ."

"It's very important. Her mother is very ill. . . ."

"Tragic," she said. She might have meant it.

"We're not sure she's going to . . . you know."

"I'm very sorry."

"Maybe one of the girls, maybe a friend of hers here . . ." Shanahan tried to look grieved. It wasn't difficult.

"I don't think so," she said. "She wasn't here long," the woman said more gently, "and she wasn't particularly close to anyone. I can't . . ."

"Did Maureen have any regular visitors?"

"As I said . . ."

Shanahan turned, looked out the door. "Maureen was devoted to her mother. And if she doesn't get a chance to, you know, say good-bye to Helen, why I don't know. It would scar her for life."

"Just a moment." The woman went into the other room. After a couple of minutes, she called him in. Four women sat around the small room. Two had been around the block a few times. One was maybe eighteen. Sexy now, though not likely to hold it until thirty. The fourth was in her thirties, pouty and uninterested. She sat examining her nails.

"I've explained the situation," the woman said. "No one knows anything, but I thought you might like to hear for yourself. A couple of minutes, that's all." She left to answer the phone on what had to be its fifteenth ring.

"Nobody knows where she might be living now?" The question met with a dumb, bored silence. "Did any of you see her with anyone, someone regular."

The blond looked up. "You sure your notta cop?"

"Not a cop."

One of the two older women got up, came toward Shanahan. "Look, we're sorry. Just don't know anything about her. One minute she's a star player, the next, history, you know what I mean? I'm sure she's a good kid and all, but she wasn't a pal. Just the way it was. Didn't want to be. Girls come, girls go. Some stick around. Look at me. I stick around like I don't gotta home. But frankly this beats putting a million little screws into a million little holes on the assembly line, know what I mean? Put a little back and someday I'll open a beauty salon."

"C'mon Roberta," the other veteran said. "The guy's looking for his daughter; he ain't asking you what you wanna be when you grow up."

"Anything, tell me anything you know about her," Shanahan said. His desperation was convincing. It should have been.

The youngest girl cleared her voice, looked around.

"Okay. I don't know anything important. Okay. But I did see her talking to this guy in the parking lot. Okay. Twice I saw them."

"What did he look like?"

She was nervous. She shook her head yes and said, "I'm not sure, okay?" She looked around again.

"Get off it girls," the blond said, blowing on her nails. "This guy's a cop or something. Maybe a freakin' weirdo. I don't give a shit about Maureen, but I wouldn't sick some freakin' weirdo after her."

The young girl looked away, forlorn.

"Well if it ain't Miss Marilyn Monroe givin' somebody the time a day 'fore her nails are even dry," Roberta said.

"A word to the wise-asses . . ." the blond said, got up, and left the room, disappearing behind a sheet in the hall.

"Please," Shanahan said, looking at the young girl. "What did he look like, the guy with Maureen?"

"Look I don't want to get in no trouble, okay? If I tell you, you gotta keep me out of it, okay?"

"Okay."

"Okay. He hadda beard."

"Yeah?"

"Okay, he was a big man."

"What was he wearing?"

"A suit—black I think. That's all I know, okay?"

"What was he driving?"

"I didn't see no car. He probably had one, but I just didn't see it."

"When was he here?"

"Couple of weeks ago?"

"Both times?"

"Both times? I don't know. Maybe once last week. Maybe Friday. I don't remember what days are which, okay?"

———

It didn't make sense. He wasn't sure he wanted it to make sense. He drove back across Washington Street, parked on a sidestreet with a view of the park. He waited. He perspired. The heat of the afternoon. No wind. The air was thick. He sat there in God's steambath, wondering why any of this case mattered. Why Maureen mattered, why his son mattered. Why anything mattered.

Shanahan noticed a kid make a third trip by the park. A car honked, pulled ahead of the kid, and stopped. Shanahan could see the driver lean over to roll down the passenger window. The fucker had air conditioning. The kid ran to the side of the car, leaned against the door, and got in. The car pulled off.

Shanahan waited. Twenty minutes passed before he noticed another kid. Tall, skinny in jeans and T-shirt. Shanahan started the car, pulled into the intersection, tapped his horn and pulled up half a block. He looked in his rearview mirror. The kid didn't move. He had stopped, but didn't move. What should he do? Back up? Forget it? Shanahan noticed a police car pass, slow down, then move on up the street out of sight. The kid started to walk toward the car.

Shanahan unlocked the passenger door. The kid leaned in. He had a feminine face, clear, bright blue eyes and deep red hair, black at the roots.

"Whatcha up to?" the kid said cheerfully.

"Looking for something."

"Something special?"

"You could say."

"Well, we could jaw for hours, Mister, but the cop might come back around this way."

"Get in," Shanahan said. What the hell did he know about picking up male prostitutes? Maybe there were code words or something.

The kid got in. He reached out his hand. "Mike."

"Shanahan." Shanahan shook on it, then pulled away from the curb and drove east on Washington.

"Haven't seen you around here before. Know anybody I know? Any of the other guys?"

"Uh . . . no."

"You a cop?"

"No."

"How come I never seen you?"

"It's not important. I don't want to do anything anyway."

"So, why are we talkin'?"

"I want information."

"You're a cop."

"No."

"Look, I don't rat."

"I don't want you to rat," Shanahan said, wondering why the kid was asking all the questions.

"You don't want dope?"

"No."

"I didn't think so. You straight? You want a woman?"

"I'm straight, but . . ."

"That's what they all say at first."

Shanahan pulled into the parking lot of a Dunkin' Donuts shop. "I'm a private investigator and I'm trying to find him," Shanahan said, showing him the photograph of Marquette. "He's not in trouble or anything. It's a long story. I just need to find him."

"Why me?" the kid asked.

"Because I think he might be someone who wants to pay for sex."

"I don't know the dude," Mike said. "So look, I'm working. Got to pick up a few bucks. If you're not lookin' for any action . . ."

"I'll pay for the information. How much do you get for . . ." he let the rest of the sentence go.

"Twenty bucks for a blowjob."

"Twenty?"

"That's what it is on the streets, man," he said defensively.

"That's fine. I'll give you thirty," Shanahan said, trying to figure out how they could make a living and trying to figure out how he'd list it on his expense report to Mrs. Stone.

"But I don't know nothing, Mister. I don't go for black meat."

"The money's yours anyway. I took up your time."

"You're all right. Listen, I know somebody who might know. No guarantees 'cause maybe this dude ain't never come down here. But maybe this guy I know knows. Name's William. Drive back, cruise around a little while. He'll show up."

———

Shanahan drove up and down Washington Street until he felt like one of the ducks in a shooting gallery. He parked his Malibu in the same place on the sidestreet, facing the park. Mike sat beside him, both waiting on some kid named William.

"Don't you worry about getting picked up by the police?" Shanahan asked. The kid didn't look like the type to survive the streets.

"They're around. You just gotta be careful."

"You ever been busted?"

"Couple of days ago. I'm a real geek sometimes. Guy pulls up. Old guy. Fat, sloppy. Can't be a cop I says to myself. Too old. We talk for a while. Guy finally says he's horny, pulls in an alley. Asks how much. I tell him and he says I'm under arrest. Just like that. So I look out the window and stupid shit that I am, I see he's pulled up against a brick wall. Fuckin' brick three inches from my face. I mean I didn't see the setup. So, from now on I'm careful."

Mike kept his eyes on the park.

"Sounds like a dangerous occupation to me."

"One time, I'm out here so loaded I couldn't see straight. Guy picks me up, offers to take me home. 'My house,' he says, 'cause I'm so fucked up. On the way he gives me this killer weed. Next thing I know, I don't know nothin'. I wake up in a gully with little cuts all over me."

Shanahan wanted to change the subject. "What do you do all day, I mean when you're not out . . . working?"

"What do you mean?"

"Hobbies, maybe."

"I got my soaps. I don't miss those. I write in my diary. I like to sleep. Do drugs. Mostly downers, though lately I been into Tallywok."

"Tallywok? Sounds like a cartoon."

"Tallywok, you know, paint thinner. Can't you smell it on me?"

"Yeah. I do. Didn't know what it was."

"Sometimes I do blues and t's," Mike said, getting bored with the conversation, looking anxiously for a sign of William.

"What's that?" Shanahan asked. What happened to the names he knew?

"Some call 'em betties and teddies. Downers. Everybody's doin' 'em. Well, not now. It's paint thinner."

"Won't that rot your brain?"

"Probably. Guys say people die from it. Slow suicide. Only I just hear about people dying. Nobody I know ever died. Hell, that cop that took me in. He smoked. That'll kill you, won't it? Smoked those funny crooked brown things. He's still living."

"You pretty sure William's going to show up?"

"Sure. Any minute now. I come out early just to beat him on the streets. Otherwise, he get all of it. I'm not as popular as he is, probably 'cause I look so much like a girl."

They sat quietly for a while. The sun just getting hotter. After a few minutes, Mike wanted to talk some more.

"What do you want to talk about?" he asked Shanahan.

"I don't know. You have a family?"

"Sure. A mom, a sister and a brother. Mom says I'm prettier than my sister."

"She know you hustle?"

"She does now. She had to get me out. They knew I was gay before, I'm pretty sure. My brother did, anyway. We're a close family, but he's in the Klan, so shit, he's gotta big problem with it. He's talkin' to me now. That's a start. So why are you looking for this guy?"

"What?"

"The guy in the picture. What'd he do?"

"A friend of his died. Somebody's got to tell him about it."

"Somebody's paying you to tell the guy. That's pretty weird. Funny, you don't look like a detective."

"Yeah, I know."

"You look like somebody's grandfather. No offense."

"That's okay," Shanahan said, "you don't look like you sniff paint thinner."

Mike laughed. "So what does it look like I do?" He didn't wait for an answer. "You know, we bought that stuff to sell it but we like it so much we're using it all up on ourselves. Shit. One thing though, you sniff that shit, the last thing you want is a cigarette. They taste horrible. So I guess there's some good to it, huh?"

"Good thing, otherwise you'd set your nose on fire."

"Yeah," Mike giggled, then said soberly, "I guess there's always that."

———

The kid beside Shanahan leaned out the window and whistled through his teeth. "Hey! Willyum! Over here." Another whistle, then to Shanahan, "the guy's cool. Never wears a shirt. Says he's a breeder."

"What's a breeder?"

"Straight, hetero. Like you. But you can't believe nobody."

From a distance, William looked like a pretty kid. Long dark hair, lean figure. Up close, leaning against the window, the hard edge showed. Shanahan figured William knew a lot about the streets. William said nothing. Mike did all the talking. Showed him the photograph.

William nodded.

"Know where I can find him?" Shanahan asked.

William shrugged.

"Thirty dollars if you take me there," Shanahan said.

William got in, shoving Mike next to Shanahan. William's only words were directional—"left, right, slow down, there, second floor, on the left, don't know the number."

———

"If you ever want anything," Mike said when Shanahan dropped them off in front of the park, "you can find me here. William, too. Right William?"

William nodded. Shanahan handed each of them two twenties.

In the rearview mirror, Shanahan watched as a car stopped for William and William went toward it.

"William's cool," Mike said. "The dude scores." Mike shook his head in wonder as William, naked and tan to the waist, hopped inside a Cutlass.

"Yeah," Shanahan said. "Be careful, Mike."

Mike smiled, waved. "Remember if you want anything . . ."

"I'm dying, Mr. Shanahan. I look at death very differently now. It is an inevitable journey, one that I now look forward to."

Marquette was dressed in pale silk pajamas and an ivory robe. He stood in his simple room—a bed, white filmy curtains at the wide window that opened to a view of downtown. There were two large chairs, draped in white. The floor, polished hardwood, was bare and shiny. There was a bureau in one corner with a collection of photographs in old intricately carved frames. It looked like an altar. The room reminded Shanahan of a chapel or maybe a monk's quarters.

"Then you know?"

"Yes, I know. I was told. I regret the way he died, but for the moment of horror, the suddenness may have been a blessing." Marquette spoke softly, slowly, deliberately. Hard to believe this was the guy in the porno film.

"Did you know he was trying to provide for you in his will?"

"He always provided for me."

"Were you aware that he was killed before he could make it official?"

"No. It makes no difference under the circumstances, does it?"

"I don't know. Does it?" Shanahan asked, trying to break through Marquette's seeming spiritual calm. Marquette wasn't disturbed. "Do you know who might have killed him?" Marquette sat down on the edge of the bed. He appeared weak. Certainly he was thinner than his image on the video. Shanahan continued. "He didn't talk to you about any possible danger he might have been in?"

"He was being blackmailed. I was the source—rather the reason for it. Willie was very frightened that someone might discover his secret. He was a gentle person, a beautifully gentle person. He was in awe of art and artists, of poets, of beauty in any form it might inhabit." Marquette looked down. For a moment, Shanahan thought he had passed out. "Unfortunately, he had a tremendous desire to possess it. It was, perhaps, his only flaw and . . . apparently, ironically, dramatically"— Marquette laughed—"the cause of his death."

"What was he so frightened of? Being openly gay is almost commonplace," Shanahan said.

"Maybe for film directors and fashion designers—and maybe even detectives—but not for someone who handles other people's money. Not bankers. Not in this city. So, you see if his secret had become public he would have eventually lost his place in the community, his income and therefore, he thought he would lose me as well. Of course he was wrong. He thought that money was the solution to everything problematical and he gratefully paid the blackmail."

"Who was blackmailing him?"

"I'm sorry." Marquette started to turn away.

"If he told you he was being blackmailed, why wouldn't he have told you the rest of the story?"

"He felt that if I knew the danger he was in, I'd be more likely to forgive the rarity of his visits."

"Did you?"

"What?"

"Forgive him?"

"No." Marquette glanced at Shanahan. "There was nothing to forgive. I was grateful for each minute he gave me. It was all more than . . . I don't mean to be rude, Mr. Shanahan, but what is it that you want?"

"I would like to find out who killed him."

"Your mission? Ask yourself if it matters." Marquette sighed. "It doesn't, Mr. Shanahan, believe me."

"It matters to his wife. She's about to be indicted for his murder."

Marquette got up slowly from his bed and walked toward Shanahan.

"This . . . is all illusion. It is. It is. We struggle on this plane. This is what we do. Tangled in a veil, we struggle. And when we hurt one another, it is because of the flailing. It is innocent, no matter how it may seem. It is our struggle to break free. This is very much like a bad dream. That is because we live in an inferior reality, Mr. Shanahan, where even in our nightmares we have nightmares."

Shanahan turned away, evading Marquette's long and intense gaze.

"Yeah," Shanahan said.

"We struggle, we struggle. We are entwined differently, we attempt to escape differently, but it is all very much the same. It is necessary pain. It is like the pain from a healing wound. It is, in its way, a good pain."

"Yeah, sort of like a tall short man."

There was a flicker of light in his eyes. "Yes, it is, isn't it? Illusion. The apparent contradiction. And no matter how hard we try to understand it, the answer eludes us. Just when we think we've found it, we are clutching a handful of air. It isn't here, or here or there. We choose to deny ourselves everything and think we can find it. Or we choose to wallow in experiences to gain the knowledge to break free. We choose to fight or to become passive. The attempts at understanding are futile. It is silly to choose. Our choices mean nothing. We must first yield to the only reality. We struggle. We struggle. When we cease to struggle, cease to expect reward for action or inaction, the veil is untangled for us. We are free."

"What are you dying of, Mr. Marquette?" Shanahan was pretty sure it was AIDS.

"Doesn't matter."

"I'm curious."

"AIDS, Mr. Shanahan. Does it give you pleasure to be right?"

"And Stone, did he know? Had he contracted it also?"

"Yes, he knew. No, he did not have it. It would have been an immaculate contraction." Marquette smiled. "Willie never touched me. Ever. He could not bring himself to *do*, only own. He was lost in abstractions. The physical world, that is the flesh-and-blood world, the world of desire, frightened him. He must have been terribly frightened during those last moments."

"I see," Shanahan said.

"I don't think you do, Mr. Shanahan. He taught me many things, introduced me to thought. I was very much caught up in the physical world and he took me over those hurdles. My teacher. It was time for me to teach him."

"He had physical desires, Mr. Marquette. I've seen the tapes."

"Of course. He was not perfect, Mr. Shanahan. I don't believe that for a moment. Nor am I. As long as we inhabit this plane, we are in danger of being tripped by the veil. It floats in a light breeze, wraps itself around our throats, our ankles, our eyes and then we struggle until we remember to give in. Or forget to fight. Whatever."

Marquette smiled again. "I'm afraid you brought the veil with you."

"Well, humor me a moment. Then I'll take my veil and leave. Mr. Stone was killed in circumstances that indicate the person who killed him had to know of a peculiar nighttime habit he had."

"Yes, I know about the nocturnal ritual, Mr. Shanahan. I don't know about 'peculiar.'"

"Poor choice of words. Meanwhile back to this dismal reality. People, even on this inferior plane, usually don't kill other people unless there is a reason. A motive. And that motive usually has to do with jealousy, revenge, greed . . ."

"Fear . . ." Marquette volunteered.

"Unrequited love. Did you kill him, Mr. Marquette?"

"This probably won't make any sense to you." Marquette turned, walked through a doorway. Shanahan followed far enough to see him go into a bathroom, closing the door behind him. He heard the water running.

"Willie and I shared something few people ever discover that they share, though I'm sure it happens more frequently than we know."

In the hall, Shanahan saw another photograph. This one on the wall beside the bathroom door. The frame was like the others. The photograph showed two older people, presumably Marquette's parents, Marquette when he was younger and a girl, probably a sister, who might have been slightly older than Marquette. Shanahan looked at the photograph as closely as he could in the dim light of the hallway. There was a long silence. Too long.

"And what is it you shared?" Shanahan asked through the closed door.

Nothing. No sound. Even the water had been turned off.

"Jesus Christ," Shanahan muttered, thinking the guy

had slit his wrists or hung himself. Shanahan grabbed the door, wrenched it open.

"Willie and I," Marquette said calmly, stepping into the doorway, an eerie back-lit shadow, "shared the same soul. We are the same person. He knew that early on, when he saw me on that ugly little videotape, when he came to get me. That is what Willie revealed to me. That he is me. And that is not as much of a puzzle as you might suspect."

Marquette stood very still.

"What about his death?"

"It was appropriate."

"Did you kill him?"

"Perhaps."

13

Shanahan wasn't glad to be home. It was the only place he knew to go. On Sundays, Delaney's bar was closed. Harry would be having dinner with one of his kids' families. The Cubs game was over and, tired as he was, he wasn't ready to go to bed at 6 p.m. Or was he? He'd been through the wringer. Maureen disappears without a trace. Frustrated, unhappy women give massages to lonely old men. Kids sell their bodies—at risk of disease, mayhem and imprisonment. Another guy's counting the days until he dies, dying of a disease that nobody cared about until it threatened the great American family. And the way the guy copes is to call the life that's leaving him an "illusion." Is he crazy? Shanahan wasn't about to judge.

Veil or no veil, somebody pulled a trigger of a gun that caused a bullet to put a hole in the brain of William B. Stone. And, for Shanahan, that was the only thing he knew for sure, that and the inevitability of his own death. At some moment, he too would merely cease to exist.

Shanahan laughed. Why does any of it matter? He laughed more. He couldn't stop. Casey was confused, barked. Einstein raced into another room. Shanahan only stopped laughing when he started to choke. Afterward, calm, he sat in the chair, leaned back and felt the rise of a sudden breeze through the screen door and heard the thunder rumbling in the distance. He looked. The sky was bleakly gray and the huge trees swayed. Wind whooshed through the leaves and they yielded. Black birds flew low, silently with the wind across the yard.

"Blow!" Shanahan yelled. "Blow, goddammit!"

Lightning snaked across the muddy gray sky. Thunder cracked behind it. Shanahan walked out into the yard and when the next clap of thunder sounded, the rain came and he screamed in delight, the wind and water battering him back against the door. Casey barked, yelped, howled—making the sounds he'd made when he discovered Stone's body.

Shanahan walked back into the gale. He could barely keep his eyes open against the wind. He heard nothing but the wind and the rain. Something tugged at his arm. He ignored it. When it happened again, he turned and saw Maureen, hair drenched, clothes plastered against her body. She was yelling at him.

———

"You're crazy," Maureen said, trying to help him take off his clothing, shoving him toward the bathroom. The shower was going, steam rising. She undressed. "You'll catch pneumonia. What were you doing out there?"

She guided him into the tub, holding onto him, then pulled the curtain behind her.

"We could have dinner in here, a picnic," Shanahan said. "It's become our place." He wanted to ask her about the empty house, about the bearded man, about quitting her job on Friday and not telling him. But he wanted her. Now. He wanted to lose himself in her flesh, more desperately than he had ever wanted anything else in the world.

He turned to face her, ran his hands down her breasts.

"What were you doing out there?"

"No, no, no," he whispered. He pressed the worry lines between her brows, trying to iron them away with his thumbs. The look didn't suit her, made her ugly. Dammit, that's not what he wanted. He wanted the tough, playful, pushy broad.

He pressed up against her, shutting his eyes. He would imagine her laughing eyes, imagine her before he knew about the bearded man in the parking lot, imagine her before he stopped believing in her. His hands went to her slick hair, then down her back, sweeping over her, grabbing the flesh and pulling her to him.

She pushed away. She looked at him, eyes fearful. She slipped out through the shower curtain. He remained a few moments, turned one of the faucet knobs and breathless, felt the sudden force of frigid water.

—————

She sat in the living room, wrapped in a blanket staring out through the screen door. It was nearly dark. The wind had let up, but the rain was strong and steady. He was ashamed, though he wasn't sure he knew why. He was angry. He understood that better.

"I thought I knew you," she said quietly, not looking at him.

He didn't answer. He tied the robe around his waist, went into the kitchen, and poured himself two fingers of bourbon. He thought for a moment, then reached for another glass and poured the same for her.

As he walked by her, he handed her the glass, then went to the screen door. He looked out. He saw nothing. The smell of wet earth filled his nostrils. He said nothing.

"I wish you had a fireplace," Maureen said finally.

He couldn't talk yet. He had no idea what would come out of his mouth if he started to speak. The rain was causing the soil to splatter the lower part of the screen. The sound of the rain and a fresh wisp of a breeze gave him comfort. He could feel his shoulders drop.

"You"—he choked, cleared his voice and spoke without emotion—"moved out."

"What?"

"Out of your house."

"What are you talking about?"

"I went to your house, Maureen," he said, still staring outside. Through the trees he could see the lights in the houses on the next block. "It was empty."

"What house are you talking about?"

"On Drexel, where you live."

"I haven't lived there for two years. Moved in with my mother. I sold the house, Shanahan. I don't know why it's empty."

"Who was the man with the beard . . . in the parking lot of the massage parlor?"

"You've been"—she shook her head in disbelief—"what are you trying to do to me?"

"Were you meeting with Rafferty?"

"Oh, my god."

Both were quiet. She laid her head on her knees, closed her eyes. Shanahan came toward her. She looked up. "Don't you trust anyone?"

He didn't answer.

"The man with the beard was my husband. He found out where I worked and came to save my eternal soul. When he came back again, I knew he'd be back a third time and a fourth time and a fifth and forever after, amen. I had to quit working there because of him. Did you know that?"

"And you didn't tell me?"

She got up suddenly, started walking toward the front door, then swirled. "I don't recall entering into any agreement about reporting the events of my life to you. Who in the fuck do you think you are? My parole officer!"

"No, I was worried."

"Oh?" she said, her voice rich in sarcasm, disbelief.

He went into the kitchen, poured more than two fingers of bourbon. "When I tried to find you and I couldn't, I was afraid." Shanahan stayed in the kitchen. "I was afraid you had gone for good. And I don't know why," his voice shook, "but that scared the living shit out of me."

When he came out of the kitchen, he didn't look at her. He went toward the screen door, changed his mind, started to sit down, changed his mind again. Finally, he stopped, looked at her. He spoke firmly because that was the only way he could prevent his voice from quavering.

"Look, could we just start this evening all over again?"

"In a minute," she said. She was quiet a moment, either working up the courage or trying to figure out the best way to say it. "Uh . . . the reason I didn't tell you I quit my job was that I thought you might think I was wangling an invitation to move in with you. I have to admit I was afraid that if you had asked, I might have said no. I was also afraid I might say yes. I was pretty sure I wasn't going to say maybe. And, pushy broad or no, I was terrified of having to decide that right now."

"I won't ask," Shanahan said.

"Despite my being a pushy broad, I'm not ready to make the commitment. Funny isn't it? When push comes to shove, I'm as flaky as the next guy."

"I told you I'm not asking."

"Thanks."

The silence that followed wasn't comfortable. If it wasn't broken, it was going to be all over.

Maureen sensed it, too. "In the shower," she said, "your face. It scared me."

"Scares me every day when I shave."

"No. I don't mean that. It was a different face. I mean really different. And I'm not sure which face you really own. I know that makes me crazy as a loon."

Shanahan sat down beside her. "The day I retired from the Army, the guys got together. They drove me to Kansas City. Took me out to dinner, then took me down to this one street. I don't remember the name of it. But it was kind of a sleazy nightclub row. We went into one place. Regular strip bar. The normal bump and grind.

"We had a few drinks and moved on up to the next place. It was pretty much the same except the girls wore black lace stockings, garter belts. It was pretty kinky. We had a few more drinks. In fact, by then we were pretty loaded. The third place, I remember pretty well. Big sign outside said Jewel Box Revue.

"Truth in advertising and all that, the sign said Female Impersonators. I tell you that because even though we were pretty sloshed, we knew what we were there to see. After the black lace, and some very expensive watered-down drinks, the guys would have gone to see a woman and mule. So it was unanimous.

"The place was pretty classy. They had a ten or eleven piece band and in our state, they sounded pretty good. A couple of ho-hum acts came on. Couple of guys, done up pretty well in women's clothes and makeup, sang some songs. Some other guy, not so pretty, came out and did one of those embarrassing comedy routines where he goes after the audience. Some pretty rough insults. Some raw innuendo. We laughed. All of us. We were having a pretty good time. The place was packed by the time the last act came on. Standing room only.

"They called it the dance of the seven veils. Because this was a female impersonator, I don't think anybody had any doubts that the person up there on the stage with neon veils wrapped around his body was a man. Not in the beginning anyway.

"The music played. The guy started dancing. There were titters from the audience. The guys at our table made some wisecracks. But the dance was long, and eventually the audience calmed down. The guys at our table got quiet, too. Real quiet, as I remember. Just watched as veil by veil came off. Finally, the dancer was down to just a few veils. Two, to be exact, one over the breasts and the other over the groin.

"The music kept playing and the next to the last veil came off. G-string. Then the dancer, in one quick sweep, pulled off the top veil and his wig at the same time. The music stopped. There was a gasp. Everybody in the audience at the same time. You could have heard a pin drop. Absolute, stunned silence. Mouths hanging open. Mine, too.

"Even though I knew better. Even though they put it out there on the sign in front. We all bought into the idea that it was a woman on stage. Of course, it wasn't. A flat-chested man in a burr. The audience roared once they got over the shock. I was shocked, too. In the Army, I had been in intelligence, sorting the real from the unreal, fact from illusion, for decades and like everybody else, I was deceived by the obvious.

"Everybody thought it was a great act, had a good time. Everybody but Krauss, a young sergeant. Crackerjack soldier. He went off the deep end. He was drunk and perhaps easy prey, but I can remember his words just like he said them a few minutes ago. 'I fell in love with her.' He was going to go backstage and kill the dancer. He was serious. Dead serious. He went to the car to get his gun."

"What happened?"

"We stopped him. But if he had somehow wandered in there alone, I'm not sure what would have happened."

"What all this means," Maureen said, with some sarcasm, "I suppose, is that I suffered an illusion or delusion or something?"

"No. What you saw, you saw. You probably saw something in me that's really there. I see you, sometimes, your face, in new ways."

"Good ways?"

"Mostly."

"I don't know much about you, Shanahan. When you

told that story a few minutes ago, I think it was the first time you talked about your past."

"I don't like looking back."

"Was it so horrible?"

"No. Just that when I'm around old people, that's what they want to talk about. So many years behind them, so few ahead. It's understandable. But, to me, if you live in the past, it's like driving with your eye on the rearview mirror. Pretty soon, you're lost. Life's out there, in front of you. Maybe here and now, but it's not back there. I'm not done yet. I want to see where I'm going."

"The cynical Shanahan is an optimist after all?"

"Never said I was a pessimist. That doesn't make me an optimist, either. I've got some irises to plant this fall and I'd like to be around to see them bloom in the spring. That's all."

"What about me?"

"I like to see you bloom anytime."

Maureen smiled, took a deep breath. "Now, do you know what I want more than anything else in the world right now?" She got on her feet.

"I know what I hope you want," he said.

"I doubt if they're the same. I want a quart of Häagen Dazs Swiss Almond Vanilla ice cream. And I want it all for myself. And if you want some, I'll be happy to buy two quarts. One for you. But if you say you don't want any, you won't get any. Because I don't intend to share even a spoonful of my quart."

"All right," Shanahan said.

"So what was it you hoped I wanted, eh? Something a little different?" She played the coquette.

"Yeah. I was hoping you'd say butter pecan." He lied. "I'll go out and get you some."

"No," she said with conviction. "You'll stay right here. It's my fetish and the last thing I want to do is swallow a little guilt with every spoonful of ice cream."

"It's raining and your clothes are drenched."

"It's my deal, I tell you. Besides, you might get regular vanilla or something. No. No way. Do you really want butter pecan?"

"No." Shanahan smiled. "I'll stick to bourbon." It was simple. She made him happy. He didn't want to think about not having her around.

"Remember, not a bite of mine. I'm deadly serious. If you don't think you can be trusted, if there's any chance you'll pull one of those sad-eyed tricks Casey pulls, then tell me now and I'll take a spoon along and eat it in the car."

"This is serious."

"Once an addict always an addict. Only Swiss Almond Vanilla doesn't cause death and depression, just cellulite."

"How often do you have these binges?"

"You mean go through withdrawal, start thinking of hijacking the Häagen Dazs truck?"

"Yeah, that."

"Once a week maybe. Only usually, I prepare for it. I buy a couple of quarts and stick one way back behind the ice-cube trays, hidden by a box of frozen brussels sprouts. I have to hide it from Mom. That way, when it's late and raining I don't have to go out on a long trek to God knows where to find it. You have anything I can wear?"

Shanahan ushered her to the bedroom, opening his closets for her perusal. She picked out a pair of cotton trousers, rolled up the cuffs and literally tied a belt at the waist. She found a T-shirt in the drawer, wearing it under one of his sport shirts.

"Looks great," she said, looking in the full-length mirror on the closet door. "Sort of a low-income Annie Hall."

"You'll find a raincoat in the closet in the living room," Shanahan said. "You want me to go with you?"

"No, make some coffee. Start a fire." She selected a fishing cap, stacked her hair up underneath it.

"Which room do you think I ought to burn down?"

"Not the bedroom and not the kitchen." She took the umbrella and raced out the front door. She was back in minutes, looking confused, frustrated. "Won't start. Water on the dispenser."

"The what?"

"Dispenser."

"Oh, I see." He fished for his keys, tossed them to her. "Here, drive mine. I got a great dispenser."

Shanahan stood at the door, watched her crouching run to the tan Malibu. In moments, the car was rolling out of the driveway. His trip to the kitchen was cut short by the loud sound of metal bashing into metal. He raced to the door.

His car was angled up on the lawn. A guy from the dark sedan with the dented fender was forcing her into the backseat of his car.

Shanahan was out the door in a flash, then felt himself losing traction. Legs out of control, Shanahan was airborne and came to an abrasive halt in the gravel driveway. He felt nothing but the need to get up. When he did, he saw the dark sedan as it fishtailed a few feet up the street, then sped to the intersection, making a right turn without stopping. All he could do was stand there, drenched for the second time in an hour, staring at the quiet street and the empty intersection.

14

Who? Why? A mad rapist? Her husband, intent on deprogramming her sinful ways? Or was it connected to Stone's murder? Perhaps they thought they were getting Shanahan and when they found out it was a woman and the element of surprise gone, they took her anyway to eventually get to him. They? Yes. There was the guy who shoved her into the car and another driving it away.

And what was he to do? His first instinct had been to go driving after them, but judging by the steam that rose from the front of the car, he wouldn't get very far. He'd already lost too much time. His second thought was to call the police. If it was a mad rapist then it might be a good idea. But what could they do without some kind of identification? Shanahan didn't know the make and year of the car, let alone a license number. All he could say was it was one, maybe two human beings in a dark sedan who took Maureen away.

If they wanted to get at Shanahan, they would call, wouldn't they? Wouldn't they? No. Nothing was certain, was it? He was no longer in control. One way or another, he had always been in control. Shanahan could either cause things to happen or—and he had a particularly fine knack to—not care.

When Elaine left, he could simply acknowledge the inevitable. Things, events, people in his world were regarded fatefully, like say an earthquake. A man cannot stop it, just hope to survive it. No panic. Resignation. Out of his hands.

It was the same with his son. If Ty chose to leave, then what could Shanahan do? He couldn't lock him in a closet, put him in a ball and chain. If he chose to live another life, what could Shanahan do about it? Nothing. Spilled milk.

Maybe it was all illusion. A tease. Just another level in a dreamworld and not necessarily a nice one. The kind of world where his wife waves good-bye and Maureen appears and disappears. What was real? His garden? His dog? Cat? A few beers with Harry at Delaney's place? A bottle of Miller and a Cubs game? Maybe the catalog from White Flower Farms? That had been enough. Why was all this happening?

Stop it, Shanahan, he told himself. No time for all of that. Goddammit, he had to play it out. He'd have to feel sorry for himself later. Inside the house, he changed clothes, his mind racing through the maze, retreating at dead ends. What had Rafferty said? Something about him not being as mean as they get. Was Rafferty on the take? Or was he simply trying to say the police could get nastier than he had been? Then again, how odd it was that the kidnapping occurred so quickly after his visit to Marquette. Even if the guy had killed Stone—and he certainly was deranged enough to do it—it didn't seem likely he'd be able to hire a couple of goons to cart Maureen off.

As far as Shanahan was concerned, the signs pointed to Kessler. But that was the problem. Kessler would be harder to get. He rolled in the kind of money it would take to buy muscle and have a bomb planted. And chances were, he'd have the connections. He might even have been involved in the Nicaraguan mess—say funding the Contras. That could have been the money going in and out of Stone's account. Some sort of laundering, hardly traceable to some unknown businessman in an overgrown Midwestern city.

When Rafferty had said this thing was too big even for him, that Rafferty himself wasn't as mean as it got, then what in the hell could an aging detective hope to do? Did he have what it took to fight against some international mob, let alone prove anything? Face it, Shanahan didn't have those kinds of connections anymore. If Shanahan were lucky and it wasn't Kessler, who was it?

Mrs. Stone? Her family had money and therefore power. She had hired Shanahan so that her denial of guilt in a court of law would have some credibility. And the old fart of a detective was getting too close. Then the poor grieving widow could still claim she hired a detective and he too was killed. Maybe the kidnappers thought they got Shanahan. Maybe they were surprised to find Maureen under all the male trappings. But now that the element of surprise was over, they'd use her to get to him. Her life for his, maybe. Or both. That was more likely.

But they were all questions, weren't they? Where were the answers? He hadn't gotten far enough in the case to narrow it down. So what in the hell would he do now and to whom would he do it?

It was their move, whoever they were. He couldn't even leave the house because they would call him. If he were to do any calling of his own, he'd have to do it now, before the goons got where they were going and decided to call him.

Shanahan reached Lieutenant Gamble at home, having found the number among those of his old euchre card-game partners. He told Gamble about Maureen's kidnapping.

"Let me know if there's anything I can do," Gamble said, "on or off duty. You're still sniffing out the Stone death, aren't you?"

"Yeah."

"Figured. And you think this is connected?"

"Could be the husband. He's a religious fanatic and didn't approve of Maureen's life-style."

"Well, let's pick him up. What do you know about him?"

"Other than his name's Robert Smith and he's a big guy with a beard, in his early to mid forties—nothing."

"Bob Smith, that's great! Gee, I'm real glad it's not something common like John Jones or something."

"Sorry."

"Well, we'll see if he fits in. One more thing, Shanahan. The maid, what's her name, at Stone's?"

"Yeah, Olivia."

"She's dead," Gamble said matter-of-factly.

"Christ!"

"Floating in the canal up by Broad Ripple. Dead maybe two hours. We probably wouldn't have found her so soon, except the rain caused the current to pick up and her clothing got snagged on a tree limb. Fuckin' beast of a storm. Some crazy housewife goes out to look for her cat and she finds him sniffing around the corpse near one of them low bridges. Freaks her out. Damn, not my idea of kitty chow."

Shanahan was barely listening. The metal maze had turned into catacombs. Hopelessness to despair. Shanahan was in over his head and Olivia had been sacrificed to his senile heroics. Maybe Maureen.

"Don't know the cause of death for sure, but it looks like she was beaten to death. Pretty bad, I hear."

Shanahan could hear the water outside, the persistant stream of water from the faulty gutter, as it spattered to the ground. Inside, the air, heavy with moisture, made it difficult to breathe and the lights in the living room, genteel before—when Maureen was there—turned shadows into malevolent faces.

"Shanahan? . . . Shanahan? Are you there?" It was Gamble's voice.

"Yes. I'm here."

"I know I've made it worse for you, but I thought you ought to know. I don't know what I can do, right now . . . other than try to find the husband."

"No, there's nothing you can do."

"You want me to come out? We can set up, run a tracer on the phone call, if there is one."

"No time. Besides, I'm sure they won't hang on long enough for that."

"I'll be around all night. Call me."

"Thanks."

"Don't mention it."

"Wait."

"Yeah?" Gamble said eagerly.

"Who knows about this—about Olivia?" Shanahan asked.

"A couple of police officers. The coroner."

"The press?"

"On Sunday night. You kidding?"

"What about Rafferty?"

"Doubt it. He's on leave."

"What?"

"Yeah, well he was acting pretty strange. Real edgy, you know? And the captain gave him a couple of days to settle down. He's pretty hot to arrest Stone's wife. The captain says no dice. He wants the case airtight. Rafferty is in a hurry for headlines."

"When's he due back?"

"Tomorrow."

"Where does he live?"

"Hell if I know. We're not exactly close friends. But I'll find out, call you back."

———

Shanahan put the telephone receiver down, moved to his overstuffed chair and slumped into it, feeling tired, old and somehow shrunken. The chair surrounded him as it might a child.

He had no idea how long he sat. He hadn't slept. On the other hand, if someone asked him what he was thinking about all the time, he couldn't have told them. He was pulled out of his zombie state by the insistent knocking on his front door. He rallied consciousness enough to go to the bedroom and pull the handgun out of the drawer.

The knocking continued. Shanahan looked through the small rectangular window and thought he could make out Rafferty's bear-like face peering back at him.

It wasn't Rafferty, Shanahan discovered as he opened the door, the barrel of his .45 aimed at the man's heart.

"I come for Maury," the man said as if he were the moving man coming for the couch.

"Come in," Shanahan said, giving directions with his .45.

"No," the man said, the voice from behind a partially gray beard sounding oddly adolescent. "Just send Maury out here."

"I said come in," Shanahan said, not in the mood for a civil exchange.

"I ain't 'fraida that." He finally acknowledged the gun.

"Well, it scares the shit out of me, so get in here before I get so nervous I use it."

Shanahan stepped back and the guy came in, looking around, like maybe Maureen was under the desk? "Where is she?"

"She's not here."

"The woman's my wife, Mister. And I intend to take her outta here."

Shanahan laid the gun on the desk, turned, looked at the stranger. "Sit down, Mr. Smith. I have a story to tell you."

"I don't like stories." Smith's eyes bore into Shanahan's in the kind of stare-down kids used in high school or maybe the kind of look he used to give opposing players at a scrimmage.

"And you're not going to like this one either, but you might as well sit down." Shanahan wanted the slob to have to get out of a chair if he was going to make a move. It gave him an edge. Shanahan didn't look at him, walked back by the desk, comforted by the proximity of the gun.

"Start talking." The guy wasn't going to sit.

"Maureen's not here because she . . ." Shanahan started.

"Her car's parked outside." Smith started backing toward the door. He watched Shanahan every second, except the one it took to verify the car was still there and Maureen hadn't slipped out while Shanahan kept him busy.

"She took mine, Mr. Smith."

"That's yours sittin' up on the lawn."

"Yep."

"Then where's Maureen?"

"I don't know. That's what I've been trying to tell you, but you keep interrupting."

"She all right?"

"I don't know."

"What the hell kind of remark is that?" Smith started moving toward him. "All you seem to know how to say is you don't know. You better start telling me what you know."

"She's been kidnapped."

Smith stopped, looked at Shanahan as if he was lying and was going to pay for it.

Shanahan told him the story. As he spoke, Smith's bravado diminished. Midway, the man sat on the sofa, head in his hands. Shanahan concluded by telling him he was waiting for the phone call. The one that would ask for money, maybe, but more likely an offer to exchange Shanahan for Maureen. He would gladly do it, but that was no guarantee they would let Maureen go.

They sat silently for nearly an hour. There was no

phone call. Shanahan saw the guy's lips move. The guy
was either praying or talking to himself, if a distinction
could be drawn between the two. Finally, the guy mum-
bled something.

"What?"

"I said, did you have carnal knowledge of her?" This
time Shanahan had no trouble hearing him. "I followed
her twice from that place. She came here. Didn't leave
until the next day. Did you sleep with her?" Shanahan got
up, went into the bathroom.

"I asked you a question."

"And I'm not going to answer it." Shanahan damp-
ened a washcloth and pressed it firmly against his face, his
eyelids. When he came back into the room, Smith was
standing, his right hand in his coat pocket; the bulge made
Shanahan a little edgy. Shanahan moved as casually as he
could toward his own gun, lying on the desk.

"I tried to introduce her to the Lord."

No good. Shanahan would never make it to the gun.
He kept walking. Into the kitchen. He poured a couple of
ounces of bourbon, took a swallow, then dumped the rest
in the sink. He had to stay alert.

"I have prayed and prayed for her. Until I was blue in
the face, I prayed for her. I prayed to God for Satan to let go
of her. Cast him out! I told her. She laughed. Look where it
got her. She committed adultery and now she's . . ."

Shanahan looked at him. A college freshman, former
jock hero who got his dream squeezed out of him. His kid
kills himself. The struggle was just too hard. The guy
made it simple. Good and evil. God and Satan. For
Marquette, the world simply didn't exist. Smith found a
rule book. And appointed himself referee. No veils for
Smith. No veils for Mike, either. The kid on the street.
Well, he just sniffed paint thinner and didn't think about it
at all.

"Sometimes I thought I should just let her go, release

the bonds. But I can't. When we married, I made a promise to God. A contract. I was young and maybe I took that promise too light, but as sure as Jesus is the way, I made a sacred vow. So no matter how many sins she had committed in the face of Jesus Christ, no matter how evil her ways, I made that promise and I owe it to Him. Please, Lord. She cannot die now."

Shanahan stared at the phone.

"Jesus will forgive her. I will forgive her," Smith said.

"You're just a couple of sweet guys, aren't you?"

Smith's prayerful eyes turned savvy and sullen. Then quietly, "You haven't much time to find Jesus."

"I'm not looking for him. I'm looking for her. If you want to stay, sit down and shut up or get the fuck out of here."

Smith's hand slowly emerged from his jacket. Shanahan believed at that moment that he'd just wise-assed himself into a grave.

"I'm staying," Smith said. The mysterious hand held a small black Bible. "I'm staying till I see Maury," he continued, some of the toughness gone from his voice. He sat, uneasily defiant, crossing his arms—a kid disobeying his father, not sure if his conviction would hold out against real punishment.

The hours in the dimly lit living room continued in silence. Smith was one more frightened and disconnected soul in a parade of them. What was scary to Shanahan, not to mention the rapid onslaught of technology and the foreign thinking that came with it, was the human debris left in its wake. No one was connected to anyone.

Not just the hustlers on Washington Street, Mike and the "cool" William; not only the women in the massage parlor having to stay a step ahead of the vice squad to preserve an anemic freedom; but Stone and Marquette—dead and dying. Mrs. Stone, rich and empty. Olivia, victim of the human storm of violence, flotsam in the dark,

cold waters of the canal. Smith, scared back into igno-
rance. Rafferty, too, pleased that his beard gave him the
confidence to intimidate, to hide the little wimp inside.
There was Kessler and his zombie family. Even if you
fought it, tried to take control of your life as Maureen had
done, you could end up in a sordid affair not of your own
doing.

Shanahan knew the list didn't end there. His name
was on it. Seventy years of plodding through little mys-
teries, oblivious to the big one. He might as well have
been doing crossword puzzles. Now there was this: this
sordid little mystery. Solving it to preserve Maureen's
life—and in a way Shanahan was only coming to understand, salvaging his own. If Marquette was right, all you
had to do was give in.

If it wasn't for Maureen, he would have. He had no
choice but to fight. He had to fight and fight smart. He
could no longer simply wait for the phone call. He didn't
have to.

"This is Maureen," the voice said.

"Are you all right?" Shanahan asked. Smith flew up
from the chair, started toward the phone. Shanahan
grabbed the .45, stopped him in his tracks.

"I have something to read you," she said, her voice
emotionless. Shanahan prayed Maureen was still alive
and not live on Memorex. "You have until tomorrow at
five p.m., to get ten thousand in cash." She read the lines
slowly and carefully. "You will be given further instructions later. Do not contact the police if you wish to see me
alive. That is all for now."

"No it isn't, tell the bastards two things. One, I'll do
as they say—anything. Two, I need proof you're alive, not
just a taped message. Or nothing. Nada. They must allow
you to say something, anything."

There was a long pause, then finally Maureen said,
"Love ya, Swaggart." The phone clicked.

15

"I'm sorry. I woke you."

"What are you doing here?" Marquette said, looking at Shanahan through a crack in the door, the chain still hooked.

"I have to talk with you."

"Now? It's midnight. Can't it wait until tomorrow? . . . Or forever for that matter?"

"I'm afraid I have some bad news. May I come in?"

"I don't want any bad news. I don't want any good news. It's a no-news day. Please leave."

"I'm sorry. I have to talk with you. It's important."

"I'll call the police," Marquette said.

"You don't have a phone."

"You noticed that, did you?" There was a slight edge of humor in his tone. "I'll scream, then."

"You may want to," Shanahan said.

"All right, just a minute."

Through the crack in the door, he saw Marquette, naked, walking toward the bathroom. Shanahan looked away. Because of the letters to Stone and Shanahan's earlier visit, he knew more about Marquette than he had any right to. Certainly more than he wanted to know.

Marquette returned, opened the door, then gave Shanahan his back as he walked toward his bed, wearing the robe he'd worn when Shanahan first visited.

"You might want to sit down," Shanahan said.

"I might want to lie down, Mr. Shanahan. I'm very tired. Please tell me what you feel you have to tell me, then leave."

Shanahan was tired too. And this wasn't going to be

pleasant. He'd done it before—in the Army—break the news of a death to a family member. Usually the person died in the line of duty. It was half expected. He'd never had to tell anybody that someone they loved was brutally murdered and dumped in the canal. Then, after he did that, he'd have to have the gall to ask this person if he'd help him out.

"Your sister . . ." Shanahan started.

"Olivia? You know her?"

"Yes. She worked for Mrs. Stone. You two were practically twins."

"Were?"

"She died . . . uh . . ." Damn it was awkward. No way to tell it, is there? He didn't know what to do. Sit down, stand up. He fiddled with his hands, then finally put them in his jacket pocket. In his right pocket, he found a tennis ball. One of Casey's. They were everywhere. He wrapped his fist around the ball and squeezed.

Marquette raised his chin as if to say "so?"

"I'm sorry, genuinely sorry." Shanahan said.

"Is that it? Is that what you wanted to tell me?"

"I'm afraid it only gets worse, if that's possible."

Marquette crossed to the bureau, opened the top drawer, pulled out a crumpled pack of Pall Malls and a book of matches. He had trouble with the matches. Shanahan offered to help, but Marquette backed away, giving Shanahan a nasty, reproachful look. With trembling fingers, he finally managed to light the cigarette. He didn't inhale.

"In some way," Shanahan continued, "Olivia was involved in the Stone thing. A witness maybe."

Marquette looked genuinely surprised. "Are you telling me she was murdered?"

"Looks that way."

Marquette looked away. "Anything else?"

"Yes."

"I don't have the desire to play twenty questions, Mr. Shanahan." Shanahan had seen this reaction before—the incredible control, sheer will holding back the inevitable breakdown. "So get on with it and get out."

"It's not that easy. I need your help."

"You need *my* help?" Marquette's face trembled almost imperceptibly. "What kind of person are you?"

"A pretty cold bastard when I have to be. Please sit down." Marquette sat on the edge of the bed. "Can I have a cigarette?" Shanahan asked.

"Help yourself. Can I get you coffee? Make you some dinner? Put on some music, maybe?"

"Coffee would be nice," Shanahan said.

"I wasn't serious, for God's sake!"

"I know. I was, though."

The silent standoff seemed to last forever. Finally, Shanahan got up, went to the kitchenette. He fumbled around until he found a jar of instant coffee. "Where do you keep the sugar?"

Marquette appeared suddenly. "Get out of my kitchen!"

Shanahan went into the other room and sat in one of the two chairs. He heard Marquette filling the teapot with water and the rattling sound of china.

"We've got more in common than you think, Marquette."

"Spare me."

"People you love, dying. And me? I'm seventy, nearly."

"We'll just have to send your picture into Willard Scott on your birthday."

"According to the insurance company tables, I've got maybe two, three years." Silence. "You hear me?"

Marquette came back into the room, handing Shanahan a cup and taking his with him to the window. "I didn't make the coffee very hot. I didn't want you to have to stick around until it cooled off."

"I don't like my coffee all that hot anyway."

"Mr. Shanahan, if you just came to chat about this and that, I'm not in the mood." His tone was softer. "Surely you can understand that."

"I do understand. So when you stop playing Mr. Cool, we'll get down to business." Shanahan got up, putting his coffee on the low table next to the chair. He walked toward Marquette. Marquette didn't turn around, just continued to stare out the window, at the lights of the city.

"It's not San Francisco out there," Marquette said.

"No."

"Not the magic. You ever been there? It's a place where you're just walking up the street, you turn a corner and there's a view to take your breath away. You could be alone there because the city loved you. Or teased you. Sometimes it frightened you. But you knew you were alive."

"I've been there," Shanahan said quietly.

"It was always there for you. The city. Didn't leave you. Didn't die."

A small shudder went through Marquette. His body bent as if someone had hit him in the stomach. Shanahan went to him, held him. "Oh God!" Marquette cried. Shanahan held him, tried to contain the body-wrenching sobs.

———

Shanahan hoped to go the distance on this one. He now knew when it would end—5 p.m., tomorrow. Today, actually. It was 2 a.m., which meant he had fifteen hours, that is unless he tried to sleep. Before he paid Marquette the visit, Shanahan had called Harry. At the moment, Harry was parked in front of Shanahan's house, ready to tail Bob Smith should the bearded, Bible-toting hulk disobey Shanahan's orders to stay by the phone. Marquette sat on the passenger side as Shanahan guided his Malibu through the quiet streets toward Fountain Square.

He had pretty much ruled out Smith's involvement in the kidnapping and the man certainly had no motive for the murders. Shanahan was pretty certain that the murders and the abduction were connected, not coincidence. Smith couldn't have been that good an actor. He had already ruled out Marquette. Even if he were crazy enough to kill Stone for some bizarre mystical notion, and even if he had been willing to kill his sister, it was doubtful he would have had the strength to beat her to death and he certainly wouldn't have had the connections or the money to hire the muscle for a kidnapping. Besides, what did he have to lose if he were discovered?

That left Mrs. Stone and Sam Kessler. It also left Lieutenant Rafferty. He remembered seeing Rafferty and Olivia talking together the day Stone's body was discovered. Maybe he was a little paranoid or maybe he was still smarting from Rafferty's physical assault. Could be. But Rafferty couldn't be trusted. Then again, it could be some other person he had been unable to link to the situation. He couldn't let himself think about that one.

Maybe time was working against Shanahan, but it also worked for him. There had been no report of Olivia's death. Only Gamble knew and the coroner. Rafferty wouldn't know—or shouldn't know—until he showed up for work Monday morning. It wouldn't be in the morning papers, so neither Mrs. Stone nor Kessler could know unless they were involved. It was now damned important for Olivia to "stay alive." And that's where Marquette came into the picture. And it was going to be Harmony's picture Marquette would be in.

With the help of one of Marquette's photographs of his sister, Harmony went to work. Harmony guided

Marquette to the chair in front of the video camera, then captured the video image on his computer monitor. Marquette's face needed little redesign. He and Olivia could have been twins, especially since Marquette had lost so much weight. The important thing was to create some bruises and abrasions.

"Back on video," Marquette said. "This isn't what I usually do. God, this is so eerie. I'm becoming my sister."

Harmony had pulled some tapes from his files and set them up on a second monitor. He then copied small sections from other faces to his computer palette and rearranged them on Marquette's image.

"These aren't the same kind of bruises," Harmony said. "These are pretty harmless, post-surgery bruises and scar tissue. But they'll do."

By the time Harmony was done, Marquette was pretty shook up. Seeing the battered image, virtually his sister's, brought everything back on him. After they got a still photo of Marquette with his head bandaged and his contusions in the right places, Shanahan dropped him back at his apartment.

"I may need you in a couple of hours," Shanahan said. "Think you'll be up to it?"

Shanahan pulled the car up, in front of the apartment-house door on Pennsylvania Street. Marquette didn't seem to want to leave.

"I'll walk you up," Shanahan said.

"No, that's all right."

"Now, c'mon. You look a little shaky."

Marquette was lost in thought. Finally, his hand went to the door handle, then he paused. "Just when you think things couldn't get any stranger, it's . . . You know, when I found out . . . I mean about me, it took me awhile to steady myself. At first, I just couldn't comprehend it. The idea of dying. Of not being here. Especially leaving Willie behind. Olivia, too. She wouldn't even be here if it weren't for me. Willie brought her out so I could have some company. She wanted to come—I don't mean to say she didn't. She was going through a pretty bad time where she was. But leaving her, it was like leaving her an orphan, with no one. So it was a very sad thing to think about leaving.

"When Willie died, I just about lost it. I guess I did lose it. But then I made believe that his death was the way it was supposed to be. I can't explain it exactly. It was the idea of the souls and it seemed right. Nothing explains Olivia's death. Nothing explains the way she died. And it's so strange that the people I was so sad about leaving have left me. Has to be something there, you know, my having to face death alone. Absolutely alone."

"It's the way we came in," Shanahan said. "And in the final analysis, it's the way we all go out. That last moment, we're all alone."

"Do you think about it?"

"Sometimes."

"Does it frighten you?"

"Sometimes. Then I start thinking. You're alive until it happens. There might be a worthwhile moment, one you wouldn't have missed for the world, so you keep living until the lights go out."

Marquette turned toward Shanahan, looked at him. He looked like a little kid. "Are you in danger?" he asked. "Do these people want you?"

Shanahan thought so. He hoped so, because that's what would keep Maureen Smith alive until 5 p.m.

"Doubt it," Shanahan said. "I'm little more than a pest."

"I'm glad I met you," Marquette said, extending his hand for a handshake.

They shook hands and Marquette opened the car door and got out.

"Good-bye, Mr. Shanahan."

"Marquette!" Marquette stopped, turned. "You're not thinking about doing anything foolish?"

"Call me Todd. No. I owe you dinner. For the way I treated you earlier. At least a hot cup of coffee."

16

Bobby Smith was asleep in his chair, the Bible resting on his chest. In his lap was Einstein, content to have one of Smith's chubby paws resting on him. Maybe Smith wasn't such a shit. Then again, maybe he was. Einstein wasn't a particularly great judge of character. Anyone who'd feed him and pet him could buy one of his nine lives. So far, he'd sold about fifteen.

Shanahan had his Polaroids. Three of them, all of Marquette as Olivia, head bandaged and a faceful of computer contusions. Shanahan's plan was perverse, maybe unnecessary and likely as not, foolish. If someone were to tell him he wasn't thinking clearly, he would have to agree. What could they expect, though? Too little sleep. Too little time. Too much to think about. Even more to do.

The next move—to be completed before dawn's early light—was a little sleight of body at the county morgue. Olivia had to die later than she did. Certainly, there had to be a question about it. The murderer had to be convinced he—or she—was in jeopardy by possible eyewitness testimony. And Harry had to be convinced to go along with the deal, that the bizarre plan wasn't caused by a gap in the flow of oxygen to Shanahan's brain . . . something even Shanahan wasn't quite sure of.

Besides crackpot schemes, something else kept nagging at Shanahan. It was Maureen's message: "Love ya, Swaggart." The most obvious reference was dozing on Shanahan's couch when he got home. Who else could she have been referring to, other than her former husband? Obviously not to God's favorite orator himself. Big Bible-bearing Bobby Smith didn't fit. If birthing Maureen into

Smith's version of Christianity were the motive, he wouldn't be asking for ten-thousand dollars and he'd sure as hell not be content to wait by the phone. For what reason, to talk to himself when he called?

Bobby Smith wasn't much help when he awoke. He had no idea what the reference meant, either. His only conclusion was that now, afraid for her life, Maureen had seen the light, opened her eyes to Jesus.

"Tell me about Swaggart," Shanahan had said to bleary-eyed Bobby Smith. "No, not the philosophy. Talk to me now, save me later. What's Swaggart's brand of religion?"

"Pentecostal," Smith had told Shanahan.

"His first name?"

"Jimmy."

"Does he have a church?"

"He travels. Coliseums, theaters, convention centers, ball parks," Smith told him.

"Where's he from?"

"Baton Rouge."

"What's his middle name?"

"Lee, same as his cousin Jerry Lee Lewis."

The answers bounced around in Shanahan's head but they led nowhere. Nothing made sense. That wasn't new, was it? It was down to this: the only way to free Maureen was to get the answer from the murderer, himself . . . or herself. And if Shanahan waited until 5 p.m., the chances were that neither he nor Maureen would live to tell anybody.

———

"I make it a practice," Harry told Shanahan, "never to go inside mental institutions, prisons or morgues. I don't want there to be a chance of mistaken identity." Both of them knew he'd do it. But what was it they would do?

They had worked out intricate plans. In one such plan

Harry was to be a corpse and Shanahan the delivery man. In the middle of the night, Shanahan would distract whoever was on duty long enough for Harry to move Olivia's body into another drawer. They discussed the idea of being some sort of health inspector. They thought about other equally preposterous plots until at last they agreed to stop playing Lucy Ricardo and Ethel Mertz and simply offer a bribe.

They were convincing. A joke on the coroner. A repayment of a practical joke he'd played on them. One hundred bucks did the trick. Harmless old codgers, the attendant must have surmised. He would be off duty in a couple of hours and there'd be no way to pin it on him. So it worked. And Harry went home to bed and Shanahan stopped for breakfast at the Waffle House, then drove out to see Mrs. Stone at "the farm."

"Why do I have the feeling you're testing me, Mr. Shanahan?" Mrs. Stone was calm, almost serene. She seemed to be more relaxed each time he saw her, and Shanahan wondered how much her husband's death contributed to her new state of mind. Then again, it was easy to relax here. Her sister's place was what some would call a gentleman's farm.

No tractors grinding away in dusty fields. No ankle-high corn crops. Just rolling green lawns. A few horses idling in the shade of ancient oak trees. Morgans, he was told. As he drove up the winding white gravel drive Shanahan also noticed small orchards off and to the rear of the sprawling home and a magnificent greenhouse to the left of the house.

"Mrs. Stone continued. "You believe I killed my husband."

"Had to be sure."

She looked puzzled, but not particularly concerned. "Are you sure now?"

They sat in the sun room, aptly named as clear early morning light drenched the exotic plants and elegant, summery furniture. Mrs. Stone had some color, apparently spending some time outdoors. No makeup. Shanahan found her very attractive. Stone's death agreed with her.

"You lied to me, Mrs. Stone."

"Not that I'm aware."

"You said you were dependent on your husband financially. I've been told that's not the case at all. That you are wealthier by far, all in your own right."

"I don't believe I ever said, nor certainly did I intend to imply, that I was financially dependent on Will. Dependent, yes. Two entirely different things. Deciding whether I wanted the bathroom rose or gray could absorb me for days, weeks. Will would eventually have to make the decision. I would be so troubled I'd nearly have a nervous breakdown. Choosing what to wear in the morning was a monumental task. I've only recently discovered that I had completely subjugated my personality to Will's.

"He was a very strong man. He had to make every decision. If I wore the wrong dress, okayed the wrong menu, I would get a considerable though gentle lecture. At first, it was what I most found attractive in Will. I had no idea that I was relinquishing my own identity little by little until I virtually lost all feeling about who I was. Who I am. Ironically, he was lousy with money. During the last few years, it was my money that kept his business going."

"To the tune of ten-thousand a month?"

"I don't know. I told my family's accountants to give him what he needed. I do intend to find out, though. Also, I'm very sorry to hear about Olivia. Please let me know which hospital she's in. I want to send her something. However, Mr. Shanahan, I am disappointed.

Throwing that photograph in front of me was not a very thoughtful thing to do. Did you do that to shock me into some sort of confession or something?"

"Or something."

"I look back over the years with Will and I deeply regret the waste. My waste. And it appears that his death . . . I say this understanding how selfish it makes me . . . was the best thing that ever happened to me. I understand how someone could see that as motive. I couldn't have killed him. It simply would not have offered itself as an option. Besides, at the time I could never have reached any sort of decision. Certainly not murder. Knowing what I know now and I don't know it all yet, I would have divorced him. But there would have been no need to kill him."

"I have a confession," Shanahan said. "Olivia is dead."

Shanahan told Mrs. Stone everything. From Stone's boyfriend to Maureen's abduction. He watched her reactions carefully. She didn't interrupt, just listened. The agony and confusion on her face was real.

"I had no idea," she said.

Shanahan believed her. Ruling out his client also meant he stood a better chance to get paid for the job and reinbursed for expenses. That was good—if he lived long enough to spend it.

———

The morning confused Shanahan's sense of reality. Hard to imagine that Maureen's life was in danger, that there had been a brutal murder the night before. Coming back down the drive to the country road, seeing one of the colts throw its head back and romp behind the long white wooden fence, the rich green of the trees and the clear sky, how could things not be right with the world? The contrast was surreal.

It didn't take long to get to Kessler's office. The office park was roughly on the same side of town. A quick hop on the loop put him there in less than five minutes.

He walked by the assistant, who started to object. Instead, she merely picked up the phone. Kessler looked up from his desk, perturbed rather than surprised. Shanahan tossed the photo down on the desk in front of him. Waited. Kessler looked down, winced, picked up the photo and tossed it back on the desk toward Shanahan.

"So?" Kessler looked toward Shanahan, but not at him.

"So. I was curious. Did you beat her up yourself or did you use your goons for the dirty work?"

Kessler folded his hands on the desk in front of him, then closed his eyes for what seemed like minutes. "You're obviously a troubled man. Do you have a family? Someone I could call?"

"Olivia is alive and will soon be able to give us the whole story. I also have the account numbers. I think they can be traced. And I think they will lead to you. So if Maureen dies, you'll be that much closer to the electric chair."

"I doubt if I'm going to be able to convince you of this, but I have absolutely no idea what you're talking about. I can only guess it has something to do with Stone's murder. I don't know the people you've mentioned. I don't know who this is," he said, now offering Shanahan the photograph, "and I don't know what happened to this person, whoever this person is."

Kessler sat back in his chair and for the first time looked Shanahan squarely in the eyes. He appeared sad. "Security is on the way up. If you leave now and you promise to take your real or imagined problems elsewhere, you can go. If not, I'm afraid I will have to file charges. I'm sorry. I wish I could help you. But there's nothing I can do."

There was nothing Shanahan could do but leave. If Kessler did it, he was one very cool criminal. Unfortunately, there wasn't enough time to pursue him further. There was one other person on the list.

"May I use your phone?"

"Sure, use the one in the outer office." Kessler's assistant got out of the way, glaring at Shanahan, then turned to go into Kessler's office. "Tell security we don't need them," Kessler told her.

Shanahan called Sergeant Gamble, asked him to make sure Rafferty was in his office at eleven. If Rafferty didn't bite, then the party was over. He had to stop by Marquette's.

17

Head bandaged again, dressed in Olivia's clothes, Marquette was nervous. He was ill at ease walking through the marble hallways of the tall office building that housed the courts, the mayor's office, and the police department. He slid into the corner of the elevator, trying to make the smallest profile possible.

Whatever he did, Shanahan told him, he was not to come into Rafferty's office until called. He was to sit in one of the long line of uncomfortable chairs and bury himself in a magazine.

Shanahan met with Gamble first, asked him to accompany him to Rafferty's office.

"What's up, Shanahan?" Gamble asked as they walked over. He brushed off his lapels with the palm of his hand.

"I want a witness."

"To what? You gonna shoot him?"

"Maybe. Maybe you'll shoot him."

"What's this all about?" Gamble was nervous. "Christ Shanahan, I can't stand the guy's guts, but he's a lieutenant with some pull and I'm a short-timer. Don't want to do nothin' to mess up my retirement."

Too late. They were already at Rafferty's door and he was looking right at them.

"Double trouble," Rafferty said with a broad smile.

Shanahan wasted no time, tossed the photograph down on Rafferty's desk. Rafferty pulled a pair of granny glasses out of the hanky pocket of his well-pressed suit.

"You're trying to tell me something, Shanahan, but I

don't know what it is. Try English. It's our common language, sweetheart."

"Looks like a photograph of Olivia to me," Shanahan said, "after a few gorillas got done using her to vent their frustrations."

Rafferty studied the picture more closely, lifted his glasses for a look, then lowered them. "My God, what happened to her?"

Gamble went behind Rafferty, looked at the photo with a puzzled look on his face. "Lieutenant, I hadn't a chance to tell you, she was found dead, floating in the canal late last night."

"Only that person isn't dead," Shanahan said without emotion.

Both Rafferty and Gamble looked up in surprise.

"She is, Shanahan," Gamble said. "I told you. Straight from the coroner's mouth."

Shanahan went to the door and called, "Olivia?" Marquette did as he was told. He walked very slowly toward them, keeping his head lowered.

"What's going on here?" Rafferty yelled.

Gamble stared, mouth hanging open.

The light from the window struck Marquette about two feet from the door and when he raised his bandaged head, Gamble let out a deep sigh, followed by laughter.

"I had nothing to do with this Lieutenant Rafferty," Gamble said.

Now it was Rafferty who looked puzzled. "What in the hell is going on?"

"Ask Shanahan," Gamble said, "this is his masquerade. Apparently he got the Olivia girl's fag brother to play dress up."

Rafferty was livid. "Everybody seems to know what's going on here, except me. You tell me my stubborn little eyewitness is dead, then I see a photograph, and now you tell me this guy's her brother. What brother for Christ's sake?"

Gamble reached in his breast pocket, pulled out a narrow, crooked cigar and lit it. There was a slim smile on his lips.

Marquette stood there, embarrassed. It was obvious he didn't know whether to run or hide.

"You know him?" Shanahan asked Gamble, but he already knew the answer.

Gamble's smile faded.

"Would somebody please tell me what this is all about?" Rafferty was all puffed up, but Shanahan didn't care.

"That cigar is quite a trademark," Shanahan said. "Met somebody you ran into the other day. Some kid on Washington Street. Arrested him for prostitution. He remembered you."

"Didn't know you swung that way, Shanahan?" Gamble said. Shanahan remembered the card games, how tough Gamble got when he was bluffing. "Got short eyes, eh Shanahan?"

"No, my eyes are fine. In fact, let me tell you a little story I see running through my mind. You're cruising down Washington Street rounding up those dangerous teenagers and you arrest a hustler and his john. You book 'em. Guy comes down maybe to bail 'em out. Big shot. Man with big money and an even bigger reputation."

"Stop dancing with the language," Rafferty said. "Get to the point."

"There is no point," Gamble said, sweat forming on his upper lip despite the air conditioning. "He's on a fishing expedition, can't you see that, and we're the fish, Lieutenant. He's out to get you."

Shanahan knew he was close. "Marquette, you recognize either of these two? It's now or never."

"This one arrested me. Contributing to the delinquency of a minor," Marquette said, nodding to Gamble.

"Sure, and the charges were dropped, so what's the beef?"

"You did a little snooping, Gamble. Free-lance. You had a few conversations with Olivia, maybe?" Shanahan *was* fishing, but he now had his eye on a particular fish. It started to make sense. Mike the street hustler talking about the sloppy cop with the crooked cigar. What was a homicide cop doing trolling the streets? That's for the guys in vice or sex offenses. Gamble either enjoyed it or he found a way of supplementing his retirement. Strange. He thought it would be Rafferty. Right idea, wrong cop.

Shanahan glanced at his watch. He had five hours. "You were extorting Stone to the tune of ten-thousand a month."

"This is crazy," Gamble said. "I don't have to take this shit." He started to leave.

"Way . . . way . . . wait a minute," Rafferty said, holding up his hand. "This is getting interesting."

"You don't believe this crap, do you?"

"Well, while Shanahan's talking, I'm learning all sorts of new things about this case. Stone was a homo, you say?" Rafferty looked at Shanahan.

"Yes."

"And he and this kid here, Olivia's brother, were an item?"

"Yes."

"Sheds a whole new light on this. New motives."

"You don't think . . ." Gamble sputtered.

"Hey, we're just here getting information, Gamble. So there is a connection between Stone, his maid and this kid here? Is that right, Sergeant Gamble? Ed?"

"Yeah. The Stone guy came down with his maid to make bail on this one. Then Stone must have used his power to get the kid out. That's all I know. I don't know what kind of trick this crud of a P.I. is trying to pull."

"Why would a homicide sergeant be out there on his own, taking in hustlers?" Shanahan asked. "Wrong department. Wrong rank. Having a sergeant doing the dirty work—that's like using a shotgun to kill a fly."

"Eat shit!" Gamble said.

Shanahan wanted to tell them to hurry up, that Gamble had also abducted Maureen. But he couldn't afford to get the police involved with the situation. They'd screw it up and Maureen would end up rooming with Olivia. The fact of the matter was that if Gamble were allowed to leave the room—two minutes for a phone call, that's all it would take—then Maureen, if she were still alive, would only have a few, precious minutes to live. In Shanahan's attempt to save her, he might have killed her.

Shanahan turned to Marquette. "The two of you were close weren't you? You and Stone?"

"Yes," Marquette said shyly, puzzled.

"The two of you were very close. Soul mates, you might say?" Shanahan's heart was pounding. He hated to do this to Marquette.

"Don't," Marquette looked pleadingly at Shanahan.

"You knew everything about him? He told you things, didn't he? Personal things?" Shanahan continued.

"This is a setup. The kid's lying."

"He hasn't said anything yet," Rafferty said. "There's some missing account numbers, Shanahan. Do you have them? Bank account numbers that show exactly where the money that came out of Stone's account went?"

Now it was Shanahan who was puzzled.

"We've analyzed the data," Rafferty said. "We know that roughly ten-thousand dollars went out every month like clockwork, only we don't know where it went. If we had the account numbers, we could find out where the money was going and we could stop picking on the poor police officer. I don't like you picking on one of my brothers on the force." Rafferty's tone had changed. There was an edge to his voice, an intended insincerity.

Shanahan reached into his pocket, found the stupid tennis ball, then checked the other pocket for his notebook. He flipped a few pages, then read off the numbers he'd gotten from the porno film. Rafferty wrote them down.

Rafferty looked up over his granny glasses. "My guess is the Bahamas. What do you think, Gamble? Is that where you wanted to retire?" Rafferty moved toward the door, stopped by Gamble. Rafferty unsnapped the sergeant's holster and removed his revolver. He kept moving, his body like an ocean liner carving its path through the crowded office. He looked funny, a big man like him, carrying the gun like it was a turd. He put it down gently on the desk of a uniformed officer. "Go read Gamble his rights. I got a couple of calls to make."

"You don't have any witnesses," Gamble said to Shanahan, then ran his finger, like it was a knife, across his throat. "None."

"If she dies," Shanahan whispered, "so will you." The desk cop was coming in.

"There's a new condition, Shanahan." Gamble spoke through his teeth, almost hissing, words coming out like venom. "My freedom."

Shanahan just stared at the sloppy cop he remembered from his euchre games. They both knew it was too late to bargain for freedom. "Two or three murders," Gamble said, "makes no difference. They're not going to burn me any faster."

"Where is she?" Shanahan asked.

"Where's who?" Gamble said with mock innocence. Shanahan wanted to punch his face in.

━━━

When Rafferty returned, Shanahan said it was vital that Gamble not be allowed to use the phone.

"I gotta right. One phone call."

"How long do you think I can deprive a citizen of his rights, Shanahan?"

Shanahan looked at his watch. "Four hours and forty-five minutes."

"Oh, it'll take that long to get the information back on the bank accounts. Then there are the questions, loads of questions."

"I got one, too. It bothers me," Shanahan said. "Why wouldn't a smart cop like Gamble make sure Stone's body was completely buried?"

"You answered your own question, Shanahan. Gamble's not a smart cop. A smart cop knows when to put a stop to the take."

"I don't buy it," Shanahan said.

"Look, maybe he thought it would set up Mrs. Stone. You know, frail housewife and all that shit. Didn't have enough strength to finish the job."

"C'mon," Shanahan said to Marquette. "Let's get out of here."

———

"I'm sorry," Shanahan said as he and Marquette walked to the car. Outside, it was still sunny. Across the street, hundreds of people at the old Farmer's Market were out getting lunchtime sun, eating, talking, laughing. Girl watching. Boy watching. "You're going to stay with a friend of mine until this thing is over."

"It is over, isn't it? I mean they have him," Marquette said, getting in the car. He looked exhausted.

Shanahan didn't' answer. He kept thinking about Maureen's good-bye: "Love ya, Swaggart." He ran through the clues again. It had to be a reference to a person . . . or to a place. Jimmy, Jimmy Lee, Jimmy Lee Swaggart. Sounds like braggart. Bible. Church. Religion. Pentecostal. Baptist. Fanatic. Bigot. Self righteous. Jerry

Lee Lewis. Jerry Lewis. Jerry Falwell. Maybe it was a street name. Falwell Avenue. Jimmy. Jimmy the Greek. Jimmy the door. Jimmy the lock. Lockerbie. No, it's too far away from the source—from Swaggart to Lock. No. He thought of Mrs. Moore, the lawyer. He was reaching.

It was like trying to remember a name of some person you knew. The harder you tried, the worse it got. A charley horse of the brain.

"Church. Pews. Donations. Collection plate. Salvation. Salvation Army. Christ. God." Too subtle. The clue was too subtle.

"What are you doing?" Marquette asked.

"What?" He had forgotten about Marquette.

"Your lips are moving, but nothing's coming out," Marquette smiled.

"You get funny when you get old. Start talking to yourself."

"What are you telling yourself, then?"

"Some things on my mind, that's all. How do you feel?"

"Somewhere along the line," Marquette said, "I had the feeling we were friends."

Shanahan looked over. Marquette's brown eyes looked hurt.

"There's some other people involved," Shanahan said. "They've taken a hostage. She's in danger."

"Someone you love?"

Shanahan was silent. Marquette turned, looked out the passenger window. "Yes," Shanahan said finally.

"Do you know where?"

"No. All I know is that it has something to do with Jimmy Swaggart."

"The preacher? What do you mean?"

"I talked to her briefly . . . on the phone. She slipped it in as a clue. A person or a place. But I haven't a fucking notion what it means."

Shanahan turned onto Michigan Street on his way to Harry's. He would put Marquette in Harry's care until he could figure out something else. As he pulled up in front of Harry's house, Marquette said, "Louisiana Street."

"What?"

"If I were going to find some out-of-the-way place, I'd pick some street very few people traveled on, where there were deserted buildings and a place that was hard to get to."

"But, why Louisiana?"

"I used to watch Swaggart late at night. He's good. Mesmerizes you. A master manipulator of the veil." Marquette laughed. "After the performance, he'd come on all teary eyed and tell you he needed your help, tell you to send money. And the address was always Baton Rouge, Louisiana. That's his headquarters."

"Can you drive?" Shanahan said excitedly.

"Yes. But I don't have a license."

Shanahan swerved into the next lane, went down a sidestreet and headed for home.

"I could kiss you," Shanahan said. They both laughed.

18

Shanahan asked Bobby Smith if there were any calls. None. Smith was eating a sandwich, apparently making himself at home.

"The cat was pretty hungry, so I fed him." Smith used his tongue to disengage the peanut butter from the roof of his mouth. "Hope you don't mind."

Smith was an easy mark. First Swaggart. Then Einstein.

The fact that the phone hadn't rung didn't surprise Shanahan. The call to give Shanahan directions to the supposed exchange spot would come closer to 5 p.m. Less time for Shanahan to think about some alternate plan. If there was anyone holding Maureen, they'd be nervous not hearing from Gamble, so he'd have to be careful.

He found Maureen's blouse, still damp from her first excursion into the rain. He opened the drawer of the nightstand beside his bed, pulled out a .45, and stuck it in his belt in back, under the jacket. He told Smith to stay there. If anybody called, they were to call back at four. He'd do anything they wanted, Smith was to tell them.

"If they want to know who you are, tell them you're my brother or something," Shanahan said. "But for Christ's sake, don't imply you know anything other than you were to wait for an important phone call. Got that!"

"You know where she is?" Smith said, washing down a bite with a drink of water.

"Maybe."

Casey followed Shanahan to the car, sniffed a frightened Marquette, then settled into the backseat, a little peeved he wasn't riding shotgun.

Louisiana was a short street. There was a three-block section downtown. Then it stopped and picked up again a few blocks east near the old railroad switching yards, ran a few more blocks, then died. It wouldn't be hard. Shanahan hoped he'd find a sedan with a dent in the front fender.

What stopped him was a tired old concrete building. Painters were outside, but they'd not yet covered over a painted sign that said Salvation Mission. The place was small. And there were people around. Didn't seem like a likely spot. Across the street was a huge brick building. In front were large neat stacks of processed scrap, the rust bright orange in the sun.

He drove through the gate. Weeds grew in the main part of the drive. Not much activity here, Shanahan figured. He drove around the building. Saw the black sedan. He pulled in near the entrance gate.

"Stay here. If you see anyone other than me come out of that building, get out of here. Call Lieutenant Rafferty. And if I don't come out"—Shanahan took off his wristwatch—"in fifteen minutes, get out of here. Go to the nearest phone and call Lieutenant Rafferty. Got it?"

Marquette nodded. "Be careful."

Shanahan pressed Maureen's blouse to Casey's nose. Then the two of them got out of the car and went back toward the building.

It was dark inside. Some of the windows were boarded. Most were just dirty. Shanahan found the door with a padlock undone. He moved quietly, hoping Casey wouldn't bark if he picked up the scent. He didn't make a sound but he picked up the smell immediately and was moving quickly up a set of concrete stairs, nose to the surface, zigzagging his body and breathing heavily.

Opening a metal door just far enough to look in, Shanahan saw a large room, windows running the length of it and Maureen sitting in a chair at the far end. A man stood over her. They were maybe thirty yards away. Shanahan peeked again. There was no other entrance except for the elevator. It was in the middle of the large expanse. No surprise there. Whoever it was could hear the elevator coming. He let the door close quietly. Tried to think.

One more look. This time he'd memorize the floor plan. There had to be a way. He opened the door about six inches. Suddenly he felt a hand on his head and, instantly, he was pulled into the room, yanked by the hair. He could feel Casey leaping over him. The dog stood snarling at a red-headed guy who stood there with a gun in his hand.

"Stay!" Shanahan ordered.

"Real good idea," the man said. "I like dogs. He makes a move, though, it's bye bye doggie."

"Stay," Shanahan said again. Casey sat back on his haunches.

"Bring him over here," came the voice of the man standing near Maureen.

"Stay," Shanahan repeated. "Stay, Casey."

Shanahan was followed by the man with the red hair. A guy who wore a forest green double-knit suit. These weren't high-priced thugs, Shanahan thought.

"It's about time," Maureen said with a nervous laugh. "I kind of expected you'd come swinging in on a vine. Save Jane."

The guy with Maureen looked pretty relaxed. If he had a weapon, he didn't have it out. A trim man, about forty, wearing jeans and a plaid shirt hanging out over his belt. Despite the casual attire, he was the slick kind. Gold chains around his neck and one of those 1940s skinny mustaches that only looked good on David Niven.

"Frisk him," said the skinny guy.

The guy in the green suit found the .45 right off, started to hand it to the skinny guy.

"You keep it. Those things scare the hell out of me," the skinny guy said. The frisker put it in his pocket.

"Bet you ain't got the money."

"It's in the car," Shanahan said. "I'll go get it."

Shanahan saw Casey inching up. Never could keep him in one place. He'd scoot a few feet, then stay in one place for a moment or two, as if he hadn't moved at all.

"Don't matter," the skinny guy said. "We'll get it afterwards. Who's the dinge in the car?"

Shanahan didn't answer.

"Don't matter. Even the money don't matter that much. It's you that matters. You trying to ruin a good thing. You two love birds gonna have to carry on in heaven. My buddy here makes great fireworks. Fourth of July. Boom!"

Shanahan figured they'd already used up eight or nine minutes. Marquette would be on his way. But it didn't seem likely they'd stay alive long enough for the police to arrive. There wasn't much on the agenda.

"Maybe I can offer you a deal. I've got nothing invested in this case. I can just forget about it. I'm just a P.I., looking to make a buck. I can come up with some money and I can keep my mouth shut."

"On your salary, you can't come up with the payroll."

"I know Gamble. He'll agree. What d'ya say?"

"I'd say maybe we're pretty stupid," the skinny guy said. "You check to see if this guy is wired. Shit, he could be broadcastin' this conversation to the world."

"Then you gotta hold this," the guy in the green suit said, handing his gun to the skinny guy.

"Shit, okay." He took it, made a sour face.

"What's this?" the guy in the green suit said. "The guy carries around a goddamned tennis ball." He laughed, tossed it up in the air a couple of times, then over to the guy with the gun. Shanahan looked at Casey. Nothing would stop him now. Casey turned a dead stop into an arching leap. With the ball and the dog coming at him at the same time, the guy was confused.

The guy in the green polyester flew backward as Casey struck him and crashed into his partner. Shanahan pulled his own .45 from the pants of the guy now rolling on the floor clutching his jaw, firing just seconds before the other guy could take him.

———

Sixteen squad cars with red lights whirling and the static sounds of police radios brought a little life to the dead neighborhood.

"We were watching him, Shanahan," Rafferty said. "The only thing we had was a few complaints that he was hitting up prostitutes for payoffs. We weren't sure. But that's why they swung the Stone case my way. If his hands were dirty in any way, they didn't want it showing up in public. And the Stone murder was sure to be scrutinized. Mrs. Stone's defense attorney could embarrass the department pretty bad. I owe you one, Shanahan."

"Wait a minute, we can straighten that out."

"What do you mean?" Rafferty asked, puzzled.

Shanahan could feel the adrenaline. It was just something he had to do. And watching Rafferty reel from the punch, go crashing back against the hood of the police car, made him feel real good.

Within seconds, Shanahan saw a rush of blue uniforms swarm around him. An arm was pulled behind him and shoved up until he could have scratched the back of his own neck.

Rafferty rolled back on his feet, straightened out his suit, adjusted his tie. "Let him go," Rafferty said.

The cops relented reluctantly.

"Now . . ." Rafferty said, with his usual dramatic flair, "does that mean we . . . that is you and I . . . are one hundred percent even?"

"Maybe," Shanahan said, smiling.

"Maybe?"

"Yeah, Rafferty. You said, 'a smart cop knows when to stop a take.'"

"Yeah, I said that."

"You a smart cop?"

"Don't you ever get tired of asking questions? You got to learn to trust, you know that?"

———

In the car, Maureen talked with Marquette. Shanahan wasn't listening. He was trying to figure out his expense account, how he was going to explain some of his expenses to Mrs. Stone. He didn't get a receipt from Mike and William. There was the damage to his car. The rental car, the dinner at the King Cole and he owed Harry a few bucks. The only thing he heard was Maureen laughing and saying, "Shanahan can be a real animal," and Marquette replying, "No, that's an illusion. In the real world, he's a prince."

Shanahan smiled. He'd enjoy the beautiful day. He honked his horn. "Look at that beautiful sky." He pictured the lilies blooming in his garden.

———

Shanahan woke up. The light drifted in through the blinds in the bedroom. He felt her presence beside him. He knew she was awake.

"Bobby and I had a long talk," Maureen said.

"Yeah?"

"He's out of my life."

"Really," Shanahan said, yawning.

"Yeah," she said. "He's converting. Bobby's decided to go Catholic. A monk, I think he said. Chastity and all that. Can't have a wife."

"I'll be damned," Shanahan said.

"Probably," Maureen said, kissing him on the cheek.

"Do you want to live in sin?" Shanahan asked her.

"How 'bout I just bring over my summer clothes? We go from there?"

"It's a deal."

———

Explaining everything to Mrs. Stone wasn't as difficult as he had thought. The only thing she really wanted to know was why they blew up her house.

"Gamble killed your husband. Later on, he started to worry about any records he might have kept. Account numbers, things like that. He couldn't chance coming to the house to look for them. He had it blown up."

Shanahan didn't want to bother her with details, but there was the matter of expenses. He was afraid that talking about Marquette would upset her. It didn't seem to bother her. Neither did the story about Mike and William. She had seen things like that on documentaries. She was a little surprised that it wasn't uncommon in Indianapolis. "Here in this city? My goodness, how things change." He thought she'd find the expenses a little out of line. She questioned nothing. Didn't even want an itemized statement. In fact, when he started talking about the money, she wanted to change the subject.

"You don't need to tell me all this," she said, sitting out on the summer porch of the farm, having a cup of coffee with Shanahan. "Just tell me how much. You've given me back by life. Mr. Shanahan, I've got to tell you . . ." He'd never seen her so animated.

"I've bought the farm," she said. "Oh, not that way. I mean, my sister and her husband are moving to Phoenix. I'm going to buy this place . . . and Mr. Shanahan, do you think that maybe Mr. Marquette would want to come out and stay with me? I mean, if we took a liking to each other? The place is just too big for one person and he sounds very nice."

"Are you sure you understand. . . ."

"I can help. Can't I? Isn't it about time I did something? He can help me. I'm very interested in Eastern philosophy."

"I'm not sure how he feels about Ouija boards," Shanahan said, "which reminds me—"

"Mr. Shanahan, I love you dearly, but you must learn to put your trust in something . . . someone."